FLASH
of Phantom Canyon

By AGNES V. RANNEY

Illustrated by MIKE STRAUSS

SCHOLASTIC BOOK SERVICES

Published by Scholastic Book Services, a division
of Scholastic Magazines, Inc., New York, N.Y.

Single copy price 45¢.
Quantity prices available on request.

Copyright © 1963 by Criterion Books, Inc. Copyright © 1963 by
Scholastic Magazines, Inc. This Scholastic Book Services edition
is published by arrangement with Criterion Books, Inc.

1st printing . . . . December 1963

Printed in the U.S.A.

CONTENTS

1805-6 Among the earliest explorers of the Northwest were Meriwether Lewis and William Clark, sent out by President Jefferson. In what was one day to become northern Idaho, they met the Nez Percé Indians, who extended a promise of friendship that was to be kept for over seventy years. Throughout their journey, Lewis and Clark were helped by the Indians, and returned to the East with glowing stories of a wild and beautiful country, alive with strange birds and fish, and rich with fur-bearing animals.

Later came the trappers, solitary men braving the wilderness for the hope of a fortune in furs. Most of them found the Indians friendly, and willing to share the country's bounty.

1836 Dr. Marcus Whitman and his wife Narcissa built their mission at Waillatpu, "The Place of the Rye Grass," near what is now Walla Walla, Washington, among the Cayuse Indians.

Near the present city of Lewiston, Idaho, at Lapwai,

"The Place of the Butterflies," Henry and Eliza Spalding opened a mission among the Nez Percés.

1843 The "Great Migration" began, with a thousand homeseekers coming West over the Oregon Trail. Most had their eyes on the fruitful valleys of the Pacific slope. Following years saw other thousands, and the Whitman Mission became a welcome resting place near the end of the long trail. The Cayuses grew surly as they watched the increasing numbers of white men coming into their land.

1846 The 49th Parallel was agreed upon as the boundary between the United States and Canada.

1847 An epidemic of measles broke out among the Cayuses, and many died of the unfamiliar disease. Troublemakers among them spread the word that Dr. Whitman was to blame. Two of the leaders killed the doctor and Mrs. Whitman; twelve other white people died before the massacre was over. The Nez Percés and most of the Cayuses were loyal to the white people; but both missions were closed.

1849 The Territory of Oregon was organized. It included the present states of Oregon, Washington, Idaho, and parts of Montana and Wyoming.

1853 The northern half of Oregon Territory became Washington Territory.

1855 Some of the tribes of Northwest Indians signed treaties with the United States Government, agreeing to cede their lands to the government and go onto reservations. Among these were certain bands of the Nez Percés, who settled on the Lapwai Reservation near the location of the Spalding Mission, and became known as the Treaty Indians.

But the Salmon River Nez Percés and those in the Wallowa Mountains under old Chief Joseph refused to give up their ancestral homes, and continued to live among the wild and beautiful mountains near the spot at which the present boundaries of Oregon, Washington, and Idaho come together.

1859 Migration over the Oregon Trail continued, so that by February 14, 1859, Oregon was ready to become the 33rd state of the union. But Idaho was still populated almost entirely by the Indians, with a scattering of trappers and a few intrepid settlers.

1860 Gold was discovered near the present city of Lewiston, Idaho, causing a stampede into the Idaho area. Mining camps sprang up at Pierce City and Orofino, and other settlements followed.

1863 Idaho Territory was organized by an act of Congress, signed by President Lincoln. It included Montana and part of Wyoming, covered 325,000 square miles and had a population of 20,000 people.

1889 On November 11, Washington became the 42nd state.

1890 On July 3, Idaho was admitted as the 43rd state.

Flash of Phantom Canyon

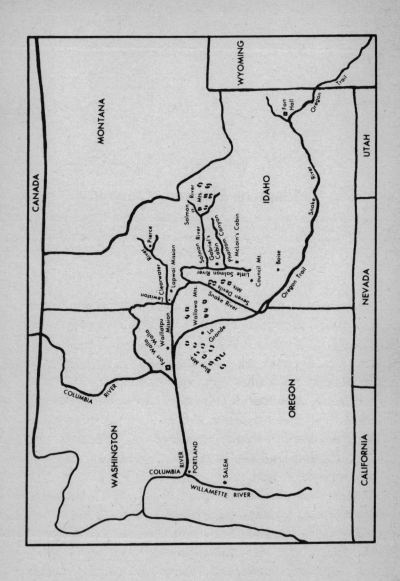

THE INDIAN CAMP

Dawn was rosy bright above the Salmon River Canyon. Crows flew cawing from their clump of cottonwoods. But rosy sky and noisy birds were lost to the boy Gabriel. He stood motionless, a bucket of spring water in his hand, gazing up the river.

Gabriel was tall for his ten years, with straight black hair and skin even a darker brown than could be accounted for by the hot summer sun. The tattered hickory shirt and the breeches chopped off raggedly between knee and ankle were plainly a white boy's clothes. But they could not hide the proud straight bearing that revealed Indian blood.

Gabriel's alert dark eyes swept the landscape — the cliffs to the east, the willow-bordered river winding from the southward. From beyond the thickly clustered willows a dozen plumes of smoke rose in the still air of the summer morning.

"You get lost out there, young'un?" That was the captain, calling from the cabin door. Startled, Gabriel jumped, splashing the cold water over his feet. No matter — his feet were bare, and the day would soon be all too warm. Besides, he was too excited to notice what he was doing. He hurried into the cabin.

"Captain — there's smoke up the river! Campfires — lots of them!"

"So?" The captain was not excited. "The Nez Percés on their way to their Council Mountain, I reckon." He filled the blackened coffeepot with water from Gabriel's bucket and set it close to the fire on the hearth. Then he opened the flour sack and started mixing sour-dough biscuits.

"Poke up the fire, young'un," he said. The captain was short and broad, with a round genial face under a fringe of dark hair. No one seemed to know where he got the title of captain. He wore a battered cap whose shape faintly suggested a uniform; that and the title were all that remained of any past glory.

Gabriel gathered the last three sticks of firewood from the basket and added them to the fire. Then he went out to where Lars was splitting wood.

"Lars, did you look up the river?" Gabriel tried not to sound too excited. "The Nez Percés are camped up there!"

2

The Indian Camp

Lars never wasted words. In silence he straightened up — a bearded blond giant, with ice-blue eyes set under heavy brows. His gaze followed Gabriel's until he, too, saw the drifting plumes of smoke.

"So they are," he said. He stooped again over the chopping block. Gabriel contained his impatience as best he could until after breakfast. At last he could keep still no longer.

"Captain — can't we go up to the Indian camp?" he asked. The captain frowned.

"To the Indian camp? What for?"

"To — well, to see them. To see the horses. We went to their camp once before, you know."

"You were a little bit of a young'un then," said the captain, pouring himself and Lars second cups of steaming black coffee. "You don't remember."

"I *do* remember!" said Gabriel. "There were drums — and — and lots of campfires — and horses."

"Don't that beat all?" the captain said to Lars. "Must have been six or seven years since the Nez Percés camped near here — they go up the canyon every year, but this isn't their regular campground. You wouldn't think he'd recollect, it's been so long!"

Lars looked deep into Gabriel's eyes.

"If the Nez Percés are still there come evening, we'll go," he said.

Gabriel spent the morning in a fever of impatience. He knew that evening, to Lars, meant any time after the midday meal. But what if the Indians decided to break camp before that? Lars and the captain pottered about the cabin, looking over their traps, although the beaver and muskrat wouldn't be fit to trap for a month or more. Gabriel tried to hurry things along and only managed to get in the way.

"Come back with that bunch of traps!" the captain called, as Gabriel carried off a bundle he had not yet looked at. A grin spread over his round face. "Haven't had so much help around here since the first day you thought it was warm enough to go swimmin'." Gabriel grinned back a little sheepishly.

"You don't need to worry that the Nez Percés'll leave this morning, young'un. They'd have been gone by now if they aimed to go today. They're likely catching a few salmon and grazing their ponies here along the river where the grass is good. They'll go tomorrow morning, like as not."

At last the meal of beans and salt pork was over, the pot scoured with sand, and the tin plates and spoons washed and put on the shelf. Now they could go! But Lars was poking in the cupboard.

"Say, I like to forgot we'd better take the Indians some kind of a present," said the captain, watching. "What've we got, Lars? Supplies are kind of low. Have to make a trip to Fort Walla Walla soon as it cools off a little — stock up for the winter. See anything at all we can take 'em "

4

"Sugar — they like that," Lars said. "Guess we could spare this little sack. We can make do with what's in the tin."

"Good enough," said the captain. "You ready, young'un?"

"I'm ready — but what can I take?"

"Oh, you don't need to take anything — this'll do for us all."

"But I want to take *something*," Gabriel said, thinking hard. He had put on a clean hickory shirt, not quite so faded as the other, washed his face, and combed his hair, looking into the scrap of looking glass beside his bed. But he wanted to take something of his own to the Indian children.

"I know!" he said, his black eyes lighting. In the corner was the small wooden chest where he kept his treasures. A collection of rocks — agate, quartz, polished pebbles picked up on the riverbank. The bright feather of a blue jay. Two robin eggs, taken from a nest deserted by the mother bird. And at the bottom, a crumpled paper bag. Gabriel took it out. In the bag were perhaps a dozen little sticks of striped candy, carefully hoarded from the bag Lars had given him last Christmas.

"Would they like this?" he asked, holding up the candy. Lars and the captain grinned.

"Reckon Indian young'uns have a sweet tooth same as others," said the captain. "Bring 'em along."

At last they were on their way, along the footpath that led from the cabin to the road. It was hardly a road, really. It was an ancient Indian trail, used in the last few years by the scattering of white settlers, so that the wagon wheels had worn a faint double track through the bunch grass and sagebrush.

As they walked it seemed to Gabriel that the men, too, were anxious to reach the Nez Percé camp. If so, it was small wonder. The Salmon River country was a lonely region in that year of 1856. Though covered wagons had been rolling west over the Oregon Trail for better than a dozen years, most of the settlers had their hearts set on reaching the Pacific slope. They had heard wonderful tales of the lush green valleys there, with abundant rainfall and mild winters. They had crossed the scorching plains and followed the wild Snake River through the hot and barren mountains of what would one day be southern Idaho.

Now they were glad to turn their weary oxen due west toward the Blue Mountains and the last stretch of their journey. If they recalled the massacre of Dr. and Mrs. Whitman — missionaries who had built the Waillatpu Mission among the Cayuse Indians — they prodded their oxen to fresh speed. A settler here and there, more hardy or adventurous than the rest, trappers like Lars and the captain, prospectors — these were the inhabitants of the Salmon River country. Gabriel had not even seen their nearest neighbors, the

McLains, a Scotch family, who had built their cabin five miles up the river the year before. Lars had visited there once, and so had the captain. But they had not taken Gabriel — and they had never gone again.

Gabriel, walking ahead, quickened his pace as he began to see the tracks of many Indian ponies. The canyon broadened as they walked, to leave space for wide meadows on either side of the river. They rounded a bend, and all at once they were right upon the camp. At the sight of the dozen or more tepees pitched on a grassy spot beside the river, Gabriel became suddenly uneasy. He dropped back with Lars and the captain.

THE WILD HORSES

THE TWO WHITE MEN held up their right hands, palms out, in greeting. A tall brave rose from beside one of the tepees and returned their salutation. The captain spoke in a jargon Gabriel didn't understand. But the Indians understood. Soon other braves came out, and there was lively talk. Bright-eyed children peeped from the tepees, but made no sound. Soon Lars and the captain were seated with the braves beside one of the tepees.

As the sun sank toward the tops of the canyon walls to the west, and purple shadows crept across the meadow, the camp came to life. Indian women kindled the fires, and soon the savory odor of broiling venison began drifting through the air. The Nez Percés were in a holiday mood — this was the time of

8

year they liked best. They looked forward to meeting with related tribes at the Council Mountain and to hunting and fishing along the cool streams.

Half a dozen young braves went to the pony herd, some distance away across the meadow, and caught their favorite mounts. Out on the flat a horse race was soon under way. Gabriel watched, fascinated. They went like the wind, those horses! Some were pintos, some blacks, some bays. But the winner always seemed to be an Appaloosa, a black larger than the others, its hindquarters spotted with white as if it had been out in a late spring snowstorm.

Tired at last, the youths took their mounts back to the herd boy and returned to camp. Lars and the captain and Gabriel ate with the chief, who accepted their present of the bag of sugar with solemn and dignified thanks.

"Better get out your candy, Gabriel," Lars said quietly. Shyly, Gabriel handed a stick to the nearest boy. The boy thanked him solemnly. Looking into the dark eyes, Gabriel was suddenly startled by the resemblance to his own face — the face that looked back at him from the mirror beside his bed.

"Why, he looks like *me!*" The thought flashed through his mind. But he had no time to wonder why — the other children were waiting for their share of candy. The shyness was quickly dispelled. Yet there was no pushing or crowding. The candy was accepted with the same sober words of thanks the chief had spoken when Lars handed him the sugar.

Soon Gabriel was wandering freely through the camp. He had seen the Nez Percés at a distance, on their yearly journeys up the canyon, and now and then when he had walked the trap line with Lars or the captain, they had met Nez Percé hunting parties. But the Indians spent the greater part of the year in the lower elevations to the north. They usually passed through this part of the country without stopping.

The tepees were much taller than he had expected, made of buffalo hides supported by tall poles. The inside was as large as the cabin he lived in. He caught glimpses of buffalo robes, beaded buckskin leggings, brightly patterned baskets of woven straw, feathered headdresses.

Darkness came on. Sparks from the campfires danced in the still air, and soon there was the sound of beating drums. The feeling of strangeness returned, and Gabriel went to sit with Lars and the captain. There was dancing around the fire. An old brave told a story. Gabriel could not understand the words, but he loved the musical sound of the old man's voice.

The sense of unreality lingered after Gabriel and Lars and the captain had bid their hosts good-by and turned toward the cabin in the canyon. The night was moonless, but the stars, large and luminous, seemed to hang just above the canyon walls.

For some time they walked in silence, broken only by the murmur of the stream and the cry of a killdeer disturbed by their approach. For once the captain was not spinning out one of the long stories he loved to tell — of China, or California, or the Klondike.

Gabriel was thinking of the Indian camp — the big tepees, the campfires, the wonderful horses. And of the boys — boys like himself, straight and tall, with black hair and bright dark eyes. Why did he look so much like the Nez Percé boys? Why did he feel such a strange stirring of excitement when he was with them? The captain's voice broke into his thoughts.

"Well, Gabriel," he said, "what did you think of them little Indian young'uns?"

"I thought," Gabriel said slowly, "that they looked like me. Why do they look so much like me, Captain?"

"You've got Indian blood," the captain said. "Guess we just never thought but what you knew that. Your father was white, but your mother was Nez Percé."

"Then — then what am I?" Gabriel's voice was troubled. "I — I thought I was like you and Lars."

"Well — " the captain began. "Well, Gabriel, me and Lars ain't exactly alike, are we? He's tall and I'm short. He don't have much to say, and I talk all the time. His folks came from Norway, way back, and I reckon some o' mine came from Ireland.

"But me and Lars is partners — and you're our partner, too. I reckon that counts more'n whether we're Norwegian or Irish or Nez Percé or whatever, don't you?"

Gabriel nodded silently, his dark eyes glowing. For a long time he was quiet, walking between the two men. Then he spoke again.

"My father and mother? What about them?"

The question fell into the silence like a pebble into a still pool. In the starlight, Gabriel could see Lars and the captain look at each other. What did they know about his parents? Neither spoke.

Then at last Lars put a big and strangely gentle hand on the boy's shoulder.

"We're your folks," he said softly. "You wouldn't be living with a couple of old codgers like us if you had a pa and ma, would you?" Something about the way he spoke told Gabriel that it would be better not to ask any more questions.

The late summer days mellowed into autumn. The captain made the long pack trip to Fort Walla Walla, crossing rivers and mountains to bring back the supplies needed for winter. Fish and game furnished most of the food for these isolated trappers, but they had to have things like salt and sugar and coffee as well.

A haze lay over mountain and canyon, and the first yellow leaves began to fall from the cottonwoods. Gabriel roamed farther from the cabin than he ever had before. Always, he watched from the rugged slopes for the feathery plumes of smoke that would indicate that the Nez Percés were on their way back to their winter home. His sharp eyes picked out deer crossing a faraway ridge, and a black bear stripping late huckleberries from the bushes on a south slope far below him. He did not see the Indians — perhaps they had made their return trip at night or in the early morning. But one day he saw something even more exciting.

The afternoon Gabriel saw the horses, thunderheads were building in the south — great piles of fleecy white, like mountains in the sky. The approaching storm that had set the crows cawing noisily had filled Gabriel with an uneasy restlessness, so that he had roamed far from the cabin.

"Sky mountains," the boy said dreamily, as he lay, chin on hands, in the grove of jack pines at the top of a steep slope above the cabin. The sound of his own voice startled him. Until now the grove had been alive with sounds — the chatter of squirrels, the shriek of blue jays, the scolding of a chipmunk. But now all was still.

Gabriel looked up through the pine branches. To the north and west the sky was black. Storm clouds were moving in over the Seven Devils to merge with the thunder clouds in the south.

He lay still, watching the gathering storm. Then all

at once, on the slope below, he saw wild horses! He caught his breath, and his heart thumped so that he could feel it pounding against the ground beneath him.

"Horses!" he whispered. "Wild horses!" He watched them come up across the slope, blacks and bays and pintos, the yearlings and long-legged colts stopping now and then to snatch a bite of sun-dried grass, the mares alert and watchful. On the edge of the herd, head up and ears cocked, was the stallion — a big bay with jet-black mane and tail and a white star on his forehead.

Gabriel had heard about the wild horses that grazed on the high mesas of the Salmon River country, and once he had caught the sound of galloping hoofs in the distance. Now they had appeared before his very eyes! He could hardly breathe for excitement.

A black cloud moved across the sun, throwing the slope and the jack pine grove in deep and ominous shadow. Suddenly there was a blinding flash of lightning. Seconds later a booming crash of thunder shook the earth. The horses snorted and jumped in fright. Then, manes and tails flying, they were running before the storm. Gabriel sprang to his feet. On ran the horses, the motion of their running part of the clouds and the mountains and the wind and the rain that followed the thunder. Up the slope and along the ridge, single file against the black sky.

14

A flash of lightning on a distant ridge beyond them threw the horses into sharp silhouette for a moment, the proud heads, the flying hoofs, the streaming tails. Then, one by one, they dropped over the ridge and vanished.

Gabriel stood still. Part of his heart went with the horses, glorying in their wildness and freedom. But in another part of him was the longing to own a horse like one of those that raced across the slope. To be on the back of one of those flying animals — the world would be his!

The lightning and thunder were not so close now, but the cold wind-blown rain beat down fiercely. Gabriel turned and started down toward the cabin, though he was sure the rain would be over long before he reached it.

He walked as one in a dream, his mind and his heart filled with the picture of the horses. Should he tell Lars and the captain he had seen them? He did not ponder long. No — it would be his secret. He had only one other. That was the cave in the bluff above the cabin.

A faint path wound up the face of the bluff, twisting and turning, leading at last to the drift of dwarfed aspen trees that screened the mouth of the cave. On hot summer days Gabriel would lie in the coolness of the limestone cavern and watch the trembling aspen leaves, pretending he was the hero of one of the captain's fantastic stories, and that this was his hide-away. But now the secret of the cave seemed pale and childish. The wild horses — he had seen the wild horses!

When Gabriel reached home the sun was setting behind the Seven Devils in a blaze of fire. The cabin in the cottonwoods, the unused and weathered log barn standing in the shelter of the bluff — they looked the same as always. But Gabriel was not the same. And something told him that since he had seen the wild horses, he would never be quite the same again.

3

THE LITTLE SORREL COLT

FALL CAME, and deepened into winter. Snow fell thickly in the canyons and on the ridges. The river froze over. Soon it, too, was covered with snow. Gabriel, going with Lars or the captain on the trap line, could hear it murmuring under the ice.

Fierce blizzards whipped up the canyon from the north, driving the snow into great drifts around the cabin until it covered the one small window and was a white wall when Lars opened the door in the morning. Gabriel helped shovel snow and cut wood for the ravenous fireplace. On winter nights, when he sat with the men in the cozy firelit cabin, he thought of the wild things. Winter, he knew, was a cruel and hungry time for many of them.

The brown bears were snug in their hollow logs or

17

rocky caves, sleeping the cold months away. The squirrels and chipmunks had their stores of nuts and seeds. But the deer and elk and antelope had to paw through the snow to the dry grass underneath, or eat moss from the trees. They had to be ever on the watch for coyotes and timber wolves. They were hungry, too, and an old or weak or careless deer was easy prey.

And where were the wild horses? Gabriel wondered, his eyes sweeping the snowy mesas. He had watched for them when he and the men had walked the trap line, but had never seen so much as a track. Had the bay stallion taken his band far down the river for the winter, where the snow was not so deep and there was still grass along the creek bottoms? Or were they hidden in some remote and sheltered canyon? Gabriel longed for spring, when the snow would be gone and he could once more wander across the sunny hillsides. Perhaps then he would see the wild horses again! The very memory of them filled him with excitement.

At last one morning there was a different feeling in the air. It was still cold. The river was still frozen. But the merest hint of the smell of spring came to Gabriel. Soon the snow would melt — he would be free!

On the high plateaus and in the deep canyons the wild things, too, caught the scent of spring. The bitter winter would soon be over. Before many weeks had passed, the southern slopes were bare. Deer and

mountain sheep began to find a few blades of grass on the sunny slopes. And in one of the canyons that slashed the mountains, a black mare left the herd of wild horses and sought a sheltered spot to bear her colt.

Phantom Canyon, it was called. But the mare knew only that the glade close to the waterfall offered safety. There, screened from the trail that wound through the canyon by a thick stand of mountain hemlock, she gave birth to her baby.

It was cold in the canyon the night the colt was born. By morning the ferns near the falls were glazed with crystal from the freezing spray. But the sun that slanted through the tree branches was warm on the colt's back. He raised his head, braced his neat little front hoofs against the frosty ground, and pushed himself to his feet. He stood there for a moment on slender trembling legs — a bright sorrel colt with two white socks and a white blaze. His mother nuzzled him lovingly, and licked him all over until his baby coat was smooth and shining.

For two days they stayed in the glade below the falls. The colt followed his mother like a shadow. He went with her to the foot of the falls when she went to drink from the pool, snorting and blowing his nose when the spray drifted into his face. His world was the little clearing, with the pale grass of early March pushing through the dead growth of last summer.

The Little Sorrel Colt

Over the cliff on the east, the waterfall poured. To the west and south was a thick growth of hemlock, while the ground to the north rose steeply to a rocky ridge. At night the rushing sound of falling water sang the colt to sleep as he lay against his mother's warm side.

Then one afternoon they ventured into a big new world. Out through the hemlocks his mother pushed, the colt at her heels. They went up the winding trail beside the stream to a sunny slope dotted with boulders. Here the grass was taller and thicker than that in the glade. His mother cropped it hungrily. The foal tried it, too, then shook his head and went to his mother for a drink of milk.

Suddenly the mare nickered. The colt looked up, strangely excited. The hillside was dotted with horses. A white-blazed bay stallion was at the head of the band of yearlings and two-year-olds, mares and colts. They circled the new colt and his mother. The foal stayed close to his mother's side, turning as the horses moved, flicking his tail when he saw colts only a little larger than himself. The mare and her colt slept that night with the herd, on a grassy slope in the lea of a tall granite bluff.

It was late — so late the moon was riding down the western sky — when the stallion's bugle call startled the colt from sleep. He felt his mother leap to her feet and heard her answering whinny of alarm

Then he, too, was on his feet. The horses were running out across the level tableland. Mares with colts were at the front and center, the stallion and the other mares behind and on the flanks of the running herd.

The horses swung in a wide arc. The gray shapes of a string of timber wolves were at their heels! Gradually the stallion gained speed, working around the outer rim of the band, turning them in a long circle to the right. He pushed against the flank of the drove until they were headed toward the slope where they had grazed in the afternoon.

The little sorrel ran at his mother's side, heart pounding against his ribs, and feet stumbling over the rocks. Down over the hillside they flew. They leaped boulders and dodged trees. The colt's sides were heaving. Soon he and his mother had dropped back until only a few of the old mares were between them and the timber wolves. He saw them clearly in the moonlight — gaunt shapes moving with the speed and silence of shadows.

Terror urged the colt to fresh speed. Then — a gopher hole! He went down hard on his side. His mother and the rest of the horses were gone in a thunder of hoofs. The nearest wolf was on him! He could see the pale eyes, the saliva dripping from the long red tongue.

Suddenly the squeal of the angry stallion pierced the air. All at once the big bay was between the colt and the wolf. His forefeet lashed out fiercely, and the animal sprang back. The colt scrambled to his feet and started after the band. His mother met him halfway up the slope, nickered, then wheeled and ran at his side.

Then, as they ran, it was dark. The walls of a rocky canyon shut out the moon. There was room for only one horse on the narrow trail beside the stream, and the colt stayed at his mother's heels. Suddenly she turned sharply to the left and leaped the narrow stream. The foal tried to leap as she did, but his hind feet landed in the water. He scrambled up the bank and followed for a dozen steps behind his mother. Then they stopped.

There was no sound, now, but that of rushing water and the hard breathing of tired horses. Close to his mother, the little sorrel trembled with weariness and fright. Moonlight filtered down through the hemlocks. The colt could see the other horses — but not the big stallion.

Then pounding hoofbeats sounded along the canyon. Ears pricked forward, the colt looked back toward the trail they had left so suddenly. In the moonlight, he saw the stallion leap across the stream and come to the band, his trotting feet quiet on the carpet of dead grass.

The colt caught the strong scent of timber wolf. He whirled in panic, but his mother nipped him to make him be still. Then he saw them through the trees — phantom shapes in the moonlight. On up the canyon, past the place where the horses had left the trail, they ran, and melted away into the shadows.

The drove was alert — alert, but no longer panic-stricken. Slowly they moved farther from the trail. The stallion stayed awake, and most of the mares. But the weary colts stretched out to rest.

As the band settled down, the young sorrel became aware of a sound that was strangely comforting. The waterfall! This was the glade where he had been born, and here the drove had come for safety. The stream lay between the horses and the trail. The waterfall threw a continual spray over the part of the glade nearest it, like a curtain of safety, washing away the scent of their passing. For now, at least, they were safe. The colt slept.

-4-

THE THREE
STRANGERS

It was early spring twilight on the Little Salmon, with the air full of sound. There was a chorus of frogs in the marshes, the cry of killdeers, the booming of a heron, the wind in the cottonwoods. Under the small sounds was the steady roar of the river, sollen by the melting snow from the mountains. No one heard the sound of the horses' hoofs until they were very near the cabin. Gabriel heard them first.

"Someone is coming!" he said softly, looking at Lars, then at the captain. Light from the fire reflected in his dark shining eyes.

His two companions looked up. The hoofbeats stopped. Then there was a knock.

"Now who can that be?" the captain said, looking from Lars to Gabriel and back again. Lars ran a big hand over his beard and spoke with his usual deliberation.

"If you were to open the door, you might find out." The knock sounded again. The captain laid down the muskrat pelt he was scraping and crossed to the door.

On the step stood a blocky, red-faced man with the reins of a roan saddle horse over his arm. Beyond him in the shadows Gabriel could see two other men on horses. The red-faced man held out his hand.

"Greetings, friend. Name's Hank. Understand you know the country around here. Me and my friends'd like to talk to you."

Soon the horses were tethered and the three strangers came into the cabin. Besides Hank, there was Wes, a young fellow with a red bandanna knotted around his neck, and Lige, an old man with a droopy, stained mustache. The captain rustled up coffee, while Lars pulled out the old chest to make extra seating space. Gabriel, back in a corner, listened and watched with wide black eyes.

It was a long time before the men came to the point of their call. Visitors were few and far between, and Lars and the captain plied the men with questions.

"There's lots of trouble with the Indians in lots of places. Most of 'em in these parts don't give no trouble, though. Some of the Nez Percés have already gone on the Lapwai Reservation, near the old Spalding Mission. Not the ones on the Salmon, though, nor Old

Joseph's band in the Wallowas. Stubborn, they are. Can't see reason. Won't give up their land."

"Doesn't sound so unreasonable they should want to stay in their own homes," Lars said quietly. Hank threw him a look of scorn.

"Well, they'll *have* to give 'em up!" he said. "Settlers want the land. It's gettin' crowded, back East and out in the Middle West. That's what I come to see you about, sort of."

He came at last to his point, and Gabriel, listening, felt chills of mingled excitement and dread run up and down his spine.

"We aim to capture a bunch of them wild horses," he said. "Break 'em and sell 'em to the settlers. There's talk of a Homestead Act. A man could get a tract of land by building on it and fencing it. Hasn't gone through yet, but they look for it to. That'll bring more settlers. Their stock'll be pretty well worn out after the trip from the East, and they'll need young stuff to do the plowin' and clear the land."

The captain rose to refill the cups. Hank sat nursing his cup between grimy hands.

"Besides, there's rumors of gold down around the reservation," he went on. "The Indians wear ornaments made of it, but nobody knows where they get it. They'll find out, though. Then there'll be a real rush for land. And these wild horses have got good blood. Appaloosas, some of 'em, from the Nez Percés. Some

27

of 'em come from the settlers that had to turn 'em loose when they couldn't make it any farther. Sell like anything, once they're broke. You help us build a corral and give us a little grub and coffee, and we'll make it right with you, whatever we git."

Tame the wild horses! Gabriel's mind left the lonely cabin, left Lars and the captain and the three unkempt strangers, and flew to the jack pine grove on the ridge far above the river. There, the fall before, he had seen the wild horses racing before the storm. He had kept their secret — but someone else had seen them.

Gabriel listened to the strangers discuss plans for building a corral, for rounding up the wild herd and breaking the best of the horses. The captain was full of suggestions, his cap tossed into a corner in his excitement. Lars, as usual, sat back and said little. The young fellow Wes and old Lige put in a word now and then, but Hank did most of the talking. At last the plans were made, and the strangers spread their bedrolls on the cabin floor. Gabriel, almost nodding in spite of his excitement, crept to bed. Slowly the fire died, and then only the stars in the spring sky lighted the lonely cabin.

In the days that followed, Gabriel watched the men with a terrible fascination. He would have searched the canyons for the horses, but Hank put a stop to that before he'd gone a dozen steps.

"Don't you go roamin' around them hills, scarin' them horses," he said sharply. "Wes is goin' a-horseback to scout out the country — he caught sight of 'em yesterday up on the ridge." So it was Wes and not Gabriel who, with great caution, kept an eye on the movements of the wild band.

The men built the corral in the grove of cottonwoods just over a low ridge from the cabin, sinking the posts deep and lashing the poles with rawhide. Gabriel watched them hang the high gate they hoped would swing shut to imprison the wild horse herd.

"Reckon that'll keep 'em in, young feller?" Hank asked. He slammed the gate with a crash that sent shivers up Gabriel's spine. The boy nodded.

"I can watch from that little clump o' thorn bushes over there, when you bring 'em in," he said. Hank scowled.

"Now, you just see here," he said, "we don't want no young'un jumpin' up and scarin' them horses, just as we get 'em to that corral! You stay right here at the cabin tomorrow — you hear?" His tone left no room for argument.

Hank and his men were gone long before dawn the next morning. Gabriel had never known so long a day. He itched to climb the ridge that hid the corral from view.

"Can't I just creep up and watch?" he asked. "I'll be still as anything!" But the captain was firm.

"You stay here like Hank said," he cautioned. "You might scare off them horses just when they got 'em going into that corral. You stay right here!"

Suppertime came, and the men had not come back.

"Wonder what's become of 'em?" the captain said for the hundredth time. "They'd had any luck, they'd be back by now!" Lars only shrugged his big shoulders.

Darkness fell, and still no riders came. Then, as the fire was dying, they heard hoofbeats. Lars stirred the fire and set the coffeepot closer to the flames. With Gabriel at his heels, the captain flung open the door just as the three riders eased themselves from their sweat-covered horses. The captain came right to the point.

"How many o' them mustangs you capture?"

It was not a good question. Old Lige growled a wordless answer, and Wes pulled the saddle from his horse in silence.

"You'll see, you'll see!" Hank said. "We'll look at 'em tomorrow. You got some grub and hot coffee? We're plumb starved to death."

Even the captain saw that questions were useless. And Gabriel knew he would have to contain his curiosity until morning.

TRAPPED

IN HIS FEW WEEKS of life, the sorrel colt had learned many things. One of his first lessons had been to follow his mother to safety in the hidden glade in Phantom Canyon, as he had done when they fled from the timber wolves. He learned to stay close to the band, to watch for bears and cougars, to find the tender grasses along the creek banks. His legs grew stronger and his feet more sure. Soon he could hold his own in races with the other colts, though he was younger than the rest.

When the herd traveled the narrow trail through Phantom Canyon to the grassy slopes above the river, the colt was at his mother's heels. They did not go down to the river — the grass on the upland meadows was sweeter than that in the swampy lowlands. The

31

horses drank from the creek that tumbled down the canyon — Phantom Creek that, high above, formed the falls in the glade.

A meadow lark sang from his perch on a dead stump that certain spring morning. Far away by the stream, a weathered cabin nestled under a clump of cottonwoods. Still farther, a feather of smoke betrayed the only other dwelling in view. Such things meant little to the colt. He grazed along the hillside, the sun warm on his back, and nipped gleaming buttercups along with tender grass.

The sudden squawk of a blue jay made no impression on the colts. But the wise old mares and the watchful stallion were at once alert. The jay screamed again. Then came the alarm cry of the stallion, and the band was off. The colt whirled to run at his mother's side — but not before he had seen the three riders that had burst from the cover of a jack pine grove on the ridge above.

With the wild band running, the riders spurred their horses, the three of them racing in a rough half circle behind the wild ones. Soon they were crowding the band, the mares with colts, and the older mares, pushing them down toward the low swale along the river.

At the outer rim ran the bay stallion, urging, pushing, guiding the herd back toward the mouth of Phantom Canyon. Instinct told him safety lay on the other side, in the glade where they had escaped from the timber wolves, and in the broken tableland and the mesas far from the river. He kept crowding the band toward the narrow canyon mouth and the rocky, winding trail.

But the horsemen were driving them toward the river, slowly pushing them down the hillside. Closer and closer they came. The colt, near the back of the bunch, could see the rolling eyes of the nearest saddle horse, a wall-eyed roan, and hear the yells of the rider as he waved his black hat in the air. On the band's left flank was a man on a pinto. On the right, a big chestnut carried another rider.

The bay stallion tried to lead his band in a long circle back to the canyon trail. But the men on the horses were fighting hard to keep them from getting back to the rocky canyon country. Suddenly the stallion changed his plan. With his rallying cry, he whirled and led the herd straight through the line of riders. The little sorrel, following his mother, made a dash between the pinto and the roan.

All at once, his mother was out of sight. There was nothing but a swirl of dust, and the rolling eyes of the roan, and the fearful yelling of the man with the black hat. Then the roan reached out and, with wicked yellow teeth, nipped savagely at the colt's tender shoulder. With a squeal of pain and fright, he wheeled and fled. Pounding hoofs behind him made him look back.

There at his heels was a yearling from the herd. Then he saw another, and then two young mares.

But where was his mother? He turned to look for her, but the yellow-toothed roan was on him. He whirled and was after the other horses.

With no leader, the colts and young mares went where they were driven — a mile, two miles — down the slope toward the river. Then along the river's edge, sometimes splashing through swampy back-waters, sometimes scrambling up rocky banks. The colt was panting and his heart was thumping. He wanted a drink, and he wanted his mother. But each time he turned to look for her, the roan was waiting for him.

The sun was hot. The colt's legs ached as his baby hoofs pounded over the rocky ground or stumbled over clumps of wire grass. For a long time they ran in the open, with not so much as a willow clump for shade. The yearlings and young mares bunched to-gether with the colt trying to keep up. And always, at his very heels, ran the roan and his yelling rider.

Then suddenly a clump of cottonwoods loomed ahead — a cool greenness in the shimmering sun-light. The colt glimpsed it between the sweating bodies of the yearlings. The riders spurred their mounts to fresh speed, and yelled savagely at the little bunch of wild horses. They reached the grove of trees. The air felt cool under the fluttering leaves.

The roan fell back, flanked by the pinto and the chestnut. But the wild ones thundered on, lured by the shade and cover of the trees, spurred by the hope of escape. Through a gap in the trees they ran, away from the terror behind them, heedless of what lay ahead.

Then — crash! The running horses struck a wall. The colt, a few leaps behind the others, was carried by his own momentum into the mass of flying hoofs and twisting bodies. For a moment there was wild confusion. Then the colt, scrambling for his life, wheeled and started back away from the wall of saplings that had risen so suddenly in front of him. The yearlings and mares were at his heels. But there was a wooden wall on both sides of them, higher than their heads, solidly lashed together with rawhide.

Panic made the colt brave enough to face even the yellow teeth of the roan. There was the opening! He spurted toward it. Beyond lay the sweeping bottom lands — and freedom!

But even as he reached it, a heavy pole gate slammed shut in his face. The black-hatted man, his horse's reins over his arm, was hastily lashing it shut. The colt reared and pawed at the poles. The gate held. Through the chinks between the poles he could see the rolling white eyes and bared teeth of the roan.

—6—

BREAKING
THE
WILD HORSES

GABRIEL CREPT from his bed long before dawn. There was nothing now to keep him from going to the corral in the cottonwoods. Walking through the coarse grass of the bottom lands, he was too excited to notice the cold dew against his bare ankles.

As he began to climb the low ridge, he could see wisps of pink cloud floating above the eastern ridges. Looking back, he saw Lars and the captain starting away from the cabin on foot. Gabriel hurried — he wanted to reach the corral before the men.

It was cool and still under the cottonwoods. On silent bare feet Gabriel approached the pole gate of the corral, put his foot on the lower rail, and quickly climbed to the top.

The corral exploded into action. Stealthy as his

36

movements were, they startled the horses. Two little mares, a black and a bay, dashed to the other side and stood looking at him, ears pricked, nostrils flaring. A spotted yearling circled the corral in panic, and another yearling, a little black with a white blaze, reared and pawed at the poles on the opposite side of the corral.

A slow grin spread across Gabriel's brown face. So they hadn't caught the leader, the big bay stallion! Not many of the band, either — just these four. He began to talk softly to them as they circled the trampled corral.

Soon the men came up. Hank and the other two on horseback could see over the top, but Lars and the captain peered through the chinks in the pole gate. Gabriel perched silently on the top rail.

Lars, tall and gaunt, stared at the four without speaking. But the captain was not so quiet.

"Big bunch o' horses! How many thousand dollars you figure to sell 'em fur?" he asked disdainfully. Hank looked a little hurt.

"No easy job to get 'em in here!" he blustered. "Like to see anybody else do better!"

"Anybody else *would* o' done better!" It was Lige, the old man who rode the pinto. "You'd gone after the rest o' the bunch, instead of lettin' 'em get away into that canyon, you'd o' had 'em all!"

"Yeah, you was bound to get this bunch!" the

young fellow with the bandanna joined in. "Dozens of fine teams to sell to the settlers, you said. And what have we got? A couple of yearlings, and a pair of two-year-olds!"

"Them little two-year-olds will make a mighty nice team — mighty nice!" Hank declared. "That little spotted pony's got Appaloosa blood — make a dandy saddle horse! And the black yearling's a nice one, too. Little skittish, is all."

It was then that Gabriel saw the colt. He had been in the corner of the corral, out of sight. But now he scrambled to his thin legs and trotted over to the other horses. Gabriel drew in his breath. A colt — a baby not more than a few weeks old! Dust and dirt matted his sorrel coat and all but covered the white blaze on his face. His slender legs were skinned and scratched, and there was an ugly swelling on one shoulder. His ribs were plainly visible as he nuzzled about one of the two-year-olds. She brushed him off and circled to the other side of the corral.

"Hey, you got a colt there!" the captain said. "Where's his ma?"

"She lays at the bottom of a draw — a broken neck," Hank said. "Tried to circle back to get her colt. Lige went after her, and she jumped one of them steep gullies. Missed her footing, I guess. So we lost her."

A bold idea entered Gabriel's mind as he looked at the orphan colt. He saw the colt grown into a sure-footed three-year-old, his red-gold coat shining, his blaze and white stockings spotless. He saw himself, grown to be a young man, astride the horse. He saw the two of them flying along the rocky ridges, over the high mesas — free as the great bay stallion and his mares, free as the eagles that soared above the canyons. So lost was he in his dream that he only half heard the arguments of the men.

"I tell you we *did* follow their trail up that canyon," Hank was saying. "Saw right where they went. There was no way out till they got to the upper end, where it opens out onto the mesa. We followed 'em, after we got this little bunch corralled, all the way up.

"There's a narrow trail in there — we figured they'd follow it through the canyon and take to the mesas out beyond. Thought sure we'd see 'em. We looked for 'em till dark, but they'd just plumb vanished! Didn't see a hair of one of them horses when we got through the canyon!"

For the first time, Lars put in a word. His weather-beaten face creased in a grin.

"Any Indian could o' told you you'd never see them horses once they went up Phantom Canyon," he said in his quiet voice. "They think there's spirits or something in there. Deer or antelope go up that canyon, the Indians give 'em up."

"Think it's ha'nted, huh?" Hank said. "Well, maybe

'tis. Them horses sure disappeared like they was spirited away."

"Puts me in mind of once when I was in the Klondike," the captain began. Then Gabriel knew he could go back to his dreaming. The captain had an endless supply of stories, and the slightest thing would "put him in mind" of one of them. Just possibly he had not actually had all the adventures he seemed to recall, but if he invented some of the stories it made little difference to Gabriel. Usually, he loved to listen. But now he was full of his great dream.

Hank and his men, too, had other things to do besides listening to the captain's stories.

"Got to get busy breakin' these horses, Captain!" he said. First they roped the little black two-year-old, and secured the end of the lariat to the saddle of Hank's roan. Then, while Wes and Lige kept the other horses crowded into a corner, Cap swung the gate wide. Gabriel's heart went with the mare as she dashed for the opening and freedom. He cringed as she reached the end of the rope and was jerked to a neck-cracking stop. She pulled back, then, fighting the rope until her wind gave out, gasping for breath, then fighting again, hoofs braced against the rocky ground. Part of the time Gabriel watched, drawn by the excitement and action. But then he turned away, his heart with the struggling horse.

"You can fill the water barrel, young'un!" Hank

said at noon, when they stopped to eat and rest. Gabriel made trip after trip to the river, lugging a rusty bucket and emptying it into the barrel the men had brought from the cabin. The horses crowded the far wall in panic as he poured out the water, but the smell drew them to it when he moved away. The little black yearling tried first, blowing his nose and snorting. Then one of the two-year-olds approached, then the other, then the spotted yearling.

But not the little sorrel. Gabriel never saw him drink. The boy pulled tender grass under the cottonwoods to tempt the little fellow, but it was no use. If he left the grass in the corral, the older horses got to it first. Gabriel could never get near enough to the colt to coax him to eat from his hand. Then he pulled quantities of grass for all of them, hoping the colt would get his share. But Hank told him to stop.

"You feed them horses so much, we'll never get 'em broke," he said. Gabriel hadn't cared much for Hank from the start. Now he liked him even less.

After a supper of beans and coffee at the cabin the evening of the third day, Hank and the others took the horses out one by one. They jerked and pulled back, then dashed ahead. But with a man to each two-year-old and Hank handling the two yearlings, they managed to keep them under control.

"We'll take 'em up the valley, first thing in the morning," Hank declared.

41

"You call them broke?" the captain demanded.

"Broke to lead!" Hank said. "Them farmers work 'em on the plow for a month, they'll settle down. The yearlings will be ready to break to the saddle next spring. Shouldn't have any trouble sellin' 'em!"

The plow! Gabriel cringed. To take those wonderful wild creatures and harness them to a plow! He longed to set them all free, to see them gallop across the bottom lands and sweep up the foothills to the freedom of their high mesas.

But it was for the sorrel colt that he saved the choicest handful of wild clover, slipping it through the chinks in the pole corral after it was so dark he hoped the bigger horses would not find it.

–**7**–

DREAM COME TRUE

"WHAT ARE YOU going to do with the little 'un?"

Gabriel held his breath, there by the corral the next morning. That was the question he had wanted to ask from the moment he'd seen the sorrel colt — and never dared. Now the captain had asked it for him.

The three strangers looked much as they had when they'd first come to the cabin, over half a month before. The old man Lige, and Wes of the red bandanna, sat their horses, the two-year-olds restless on their ropes. Hank stood with the roan's reins over his arm, the yearlings' lead ropes fastened to the saddle horn. And alone in the trampled, dusty corral the sorrel colt stood on spindly legs, his stubby, matted tail twitching back and forth in a hopeless effort to drive away the flies.

43

"Put a rope on him and take him along, I reckon," Hank said, answering the captain's question. "Ought to be worth ten-fifteen dollars." Old Lige snorted.

"Think anybody's fool enough to pay money for a runt like that? His ribs stick out like a washboard. They'd have to feed him two-three years 'fore they could work 'im. You drag him up the valley at the end of a rope, he'll be dead by night, anyway."

"Yeah," said Wes, as the black two-year-old jerked at her rope, "ain't we got enough trouble without draggin' him along? Be different if his ma was here. Then he'd foller with no trouble." Hank shrugged.

"All right, then," he said. "What do you say we do with 'im? Turn 'im loose? Or shoot 'im?"

"Turn him loose," said Wes.

"For the coyotes, or b'ar?" asked Lige. "Ain't you got no feelin's at all?"

A lump filled Gabriel's throat. He thought he was going to choke. He gulped. Then he edged along the side of the corral until he stood close to Hank. The men took no notice of him. Finally he gave a tug on Hank's grimy shirt sleeve and the man looked down.

"If you don't want him — " Gabriel caught his breath and started over, "if you don't want him — can I have him?"

"You?" Yank guffawed. "How much you aim to offer fer 'im?" Gabriel blinked. "How much money you got?" Hank prodded.

44

"Money? I — I don't have money."

Gabriel felt his face grow hot. The request that had seemed so reasonable suddenly sounded ridiculous. All the men were looking at him. He looked down at his bare feet beneath the tattered breeches. How had he dared to think the men would give him the golden colt?

"You got no money, you can't talk horse buyin'," Hank said. "We'll put a rope on 'im — we can't lose nothin' by tryin' 'im out."

He tied the two restless yearlings to the gate post, mounted, and started toward the end of the corral where the colt stood. At sight of the roan, the little one wheeled in fright and circled the corral.

Suddenly the rope spun out and the loop settled around the colt's neck. Back against the noose he jerked and pulled, fighting with all his strength. Small hoofs braced, he pulled until his eyes glazed and his limbs trembled. Then a gasp for breath and a dash in the other direction, only to crash into the poles of the corral. Pull and tug again, while Hank shortened the rope, dragging him nearer the roan.

Gabriel, on the gate, crammed the back of his hand against his mouth. He could not look — but he could not stop looking. Closer and closer to the roan Hank dragged the colt. Still he fought. Suddenly, with eyes rolling, the roan reached out and gave the colt's back a vicious bite.

It was too much. Gabriel tumbled off the gate and flew across the corral. He faced the roan with a fury of battering fists.

"Don't! Don't!" he screamed.

The roan reared back, startled as if a rabbit had sprung out of the brush at his feet.

"What you doin' there, you idiot young'un?" Hank shouted. Then the stretched rope caught Gabriel across the ankles. He landed on his back with a thud.

For a moment things went black. Then Lars was dragging him away from the roan.

"That horse could kill you, don't you know that? You stay there!" he growled at the boy, setting him down at the edge of the corral. He turned to Hank.

"Stop it!" he shouted. "Let that colt go!" There was thunder in his voice. Gabriel had never heard him sound like that. Hank slacked up on the rope. The colt stood trembling.

"Why?" demanded Hank. "Why should I?"

"He belongs to the boy, that's why!"

"How so?" Hank blustered. "He's got no money to pay for 'im!"

"He's earned him, packing water up here for these horses, pulling grass for 'em, with never so much as a thank ye!"

Hank shrugged. "Pretty high and mighty," he grumbled. "But have it your own way. He's nothin' but a runt, anyway — probably never raise 'im."

46

He dismounted and inched his way down the rope toward the colt, who flew back in fresh panic as he approached. But at last the rope was loosened. The colt jerked his head free and skittered to the farthest edge of the corral.

Gabriel couldn't speak. Only the gaze from the depths of his dark eyes to those of Lars expressed his feelings.

-8-

FLASH AND
THE McLAINS

THE MEN WERE GONE. Gabriel had hardly noticed when they left, with the half-broken wild horses pulling back on their lead ropes or dashing ahead to entangle the saddle horses. The boy's whole thought was of the colt.

"What you going to call 'im?" the captain asked, grinning. Gabriel knew the colt's name, though he had never said it aloud even to himself. He had known it since the day he saw the wild horses with the lightning dancing along the ridges beyond them.

"His name is Flash," he said.

"Flash!" snorted the captain. "He don't look so flashy to me! Look at 'im — ribs stickin' out, big bump on his shoulder, legs skinned up, flies all over 'im — "

"But he will!" Gabriel cried. "I'll brush him, and — "

"Better feed him first, looks like," Lars said. "He needs his ma — or some milk from somewhere else, seein' she's gone. Little thing is just a bag of bones."

Milk? Where could he get milk? Gabriel didn't even know the taste of milk. He drank water or else a diluted version of the captain's black brew. Why, he'd hardly even seen a cow! Unless — unless —

"I know who has a cow!" he burst out. "The new settlers up the river! You said so, Captain, when you went up there! Maybe I can get some milk from them!"

Lars and the captain exchanged glances. The captain shook his head.

"Wouldn't ask 'em if I was you," he said. "Mr. McLain don't like Injuns. Plumb set agin 'em, I hear."

"But Flash has to have milk. He won't eat grass, and I haven't even seen him drink water — though I s'pose he does at night when no one is around. Can't I ask 'em?"

"McLain's dead set agin Injuns," the captain repeated.

"He wouldn't hurt a young'un," Lars said. "His missus is a good woman — she wouldn't let harm come to the little feller. Let the boy try." The captain shrugged his shoulders.

"Don't say you weren't warned," he said, half to Lars and half to Gabriel. But Gabriel didn't hear. He was already off through the trees and on the way to the cabin.

Sweat was trickling between his bony shoulder blades when he reached it, but Gabriel didn't give a thought to the heat. One thing he needed — something to carry home the milk he was so sure the neighbors would give him for Flash.

There wasn't much choice. He poked about among the few cooking utensils. A stone crock? A rusty tin pail? There wasn't much else besides the three-legged pot which held the remains of last night's beans and the blackened Dutch oven in which a few fragments of sour-dough bread were drying in the heat of the little cabin.

Gabriel decided on the crock. It would be harder to carry, but it would keep the milk cooler in the hot sun. He saw the captain and Lars sauntering toward the cabin when he glanced back from the end of the path. Then he turned onto the dim wagon trail that led up the valley.

It was hot. The sun beat down into the valley and danced back into Gabriel's eyes from the river that roughly followed the road. The willows that grew along the riverbanks were too short to give much shade. But Gabriel didn't mind.

The colt! At last the colt was his!

"Flash!" he said aloud, thrilling at the name. "Flash!"

But now Flash needed milk. He must hurry. His bare feet kicked up little puffs of dust as he trotted along one track of the wagon trail.

The valley broadened with each passing mile. Gabriel noted the blackened circles where the Indian campfires had been the fall before. Far up the valley, he could see a tiny moving cloud of dust. That would be Hank and his men, with the horses they hoped to sell to the settlers.

A mile or so ahead and to his left, a plume of smoke arose, drifting up through the cottonwoods that hid the McLain cabin. There had been a good deal of talk the fall before when the McLains had arrived. The captain had said it was a fine thing to have neighbors. Gabriel wondered why Lars and the captain had never gone back after that first visit — and why they had not taken him with them.

What had the captain said about Mr. McLain? Gabriel mulled it over in his mind as he turned off on the dimmer wagon track that angled across toward the cottonwood grove. He didn't like Indians? But Gabriel wasn't — yes, he *was* part Indian. Did that mean the neighbors wouldn't like *him?*

Gabriel's pace had slowed to a walk. Now, as he came closer to the cottonwoods, his feet moved even more reluctantly.

It was cooler when he reached the trees. He could see the cabin now — well built, the ends of the logs barely weathered by their first winter. There was a big log barn, too, and a rail corral with a saddle horse tied at the gate. A red rooster crowed from the fence top, and a hen scratched busily in the dooryard, surrounded by her brood. Gabriel, fascinated, squatted on his heels to watch them.

"What ye doing here?" The voice was gruff. Gabriel started and jumped to his feet, hugging the crock. In the cabin doorway stood a giant of a man — Mr. McLain, he guessed — broad-shouldered, red-faced, with curly black hair. A scowl knitted his brows. Gabriel was tempted to turn and run. Then he thought of hungry little Flash back in the corral.

"I — I came to get some mlk for my colt," he said.

"Milk, is it? Well, ye've come to the wrong place. Now be off." He moved toward Gabriel with a sweeping movement of his hand toward the road.

"Who is it, Mac?" A woman appeared in the doorway, her hands covered with flour. "Why, it's a lad! Where did you come from, boy?" Gabriel looked at the round, pleasant face, the smooth forehead beneath the neat brown hair, the dark dress, and the clean white apron. He also saw the smile in the deep blue eyes.

"I came from down the river," he said, "and I'd like to get some milk for my colt. His ma's dead and

52

he's hungry. He won't eat grass, and if he doesn't get some milk he'll — he'll — " He stopped, out of breath.

"I should think we could spare the little thing a wee drop of milk," said Mrs. McLain. "Just let me get my bread kneaded down and covered, and we'll see about it."

"Are ye out of your wits?" shouted her husband. "He's an Indian!"

"He's a wee lad and he's got a baby colt that needs milk. There's no harm in giving a helping hand." Mrs. McLain's voice was calm, in contrast to her husband's bluster.

"I tell ye he's a savage! They're not to be trusted!"

A savage? The word made Gabriel think of a vicious animal. What did the man mean, calling him a savage, when he only wanted food for a starving colt? Gabriel shrank back a little, half frightened, half angry.

Mac towered over his wife. But she stepped up to him, blue eyes flashing.

"Now, Mac, I'd be ashamed to admit I was afraid of a lad that came no higher than my britches top, a great man like you!" she snapped. "He'll have his milk, and I'll hear no more about it!" She went back to her bread and pummeled it with vigor.

A girl no larger than Gabriel appeared from another room, her eyes round with curiosity, a chubby baby boy in her arms. Gabriel stood first on one foot and then the other as Mrs. McLain kneaded her bread. Mac's face became a deeper shade of red.

"How's the milk to be paid for?" he demanded. "Did you bring money to pay for it?"

Money? *That* again! That's what Hank had asked him when he'd asked for the colt. Of course he had no money. He stood silently.

"Speak up! If you've no money you'd better be on your way! Ye can't mean to *give* the milk away, Sarah?"

"There must be," thought Gabriel desperately, "there just must be some way to get the milk for Flash. Lars had been there, before, to come to his rescue. But Lars hadn't paid for the colt. Gabriel had done that, himself, watering the horses and pulling grass for them. That was it! He drew himself up.

"I'll work for it!" he said proudly.

"Work, is it?" said Mac scornfully. "What sort of work could ye do?"

"He could do plenty of work!" Mrs. McLain said as she wiped her hands. "There's the garden to be weeded and wood to be cut. Don't tell me there's no work he could do!"

"Suit yourself. But he's an Indian, and don't you forget it!" Mac turned and went to the corral, untied the saddle horse, and rode off through the cotton-woods toward the open field between the river and the wooded foothills. Mrs. McLain gazed after him.

"Stubborn," she said, as if to herself. "A fine man, but stubborn." She turned to Gabriel.

"Well, come along," she said, "let's get your milk." She led the way to the covered well in the yard, turned the crank on a windlass, and drew up a damp wooden bucket. From it she took a crock larger than the one Gabriel held, and poured into his a generous amount of creamy milk. The girl and the baby watched silently from the doorway.

"How are you going to feed it to the wee thing?" Mrs. McLain asked.

"I — I don't know. Wont' he just drink it?" asked Gabriel.

"He's used to sucking, you know. 'Twould take some time to teach him to drink from a pail. Jean, get one of the bottles we use for the lambs," she said to the girl. "Here, give Brian to me."

The baby held out his arms as his mother took him, and Jean ran to the barn, brown braids flying. Soon she was back with a big brown bottle fitted with a heavy rubber nipple.

"Sometimes the ewes won't take their babies, and we have to feed them by hand," explained Mrs. McLain. "We only have a few so far — and a job it was to get them here. But Mac thinks this will be fine country for sheep. You can use the bottle to feed your colt," she went on. "What shall we call you, lad?"

"My name is Gabriel," said the boy. The woman's brows arched in surprise.

"That's a good Bible name," she said. "Well, run along with your milk, Gabriel, and good luck with your baby!"

"What shall I do for the milk?" Gabriel asked.

"Do? Oh, to pay for it? Well, you'd best not wait today, lad. Go feed the little fellow. You'll be needing more milk tomorrow — you can make up for it then. But wait — have a drink of buttermilk and a scone before you go. Jean, bring a cup and then go butter a scone for Gabriel."

Gabriel had never tasted anything so delicious as the cool buttermilk Mrs. McLain poured from a smaller crock before she lowered the bucket back into the coolness of the well. And he had never tasted anything like the sweet crumbly scone that Jean shyly thrust toward him. It looked a little like the captain's sour-dough biscuits but tasted a hundred times better.

He started back down the road, his arms around the precious crock of milk, and his head buzzing with new and exciting thoughts.

GABRIEL'S
PATIENCE
REWARDED

Here, Flash! Here, little feller. Come and get it!"
In the corral that afternoon, Gabriel talked softly
to the colt and held out the bottle of milk. Cautiously
he walked toward Flash. A step, two steps. Then, with
a flick of his tail, the colt skittered to the far side of the
corral.

"Why won't he drink?" There was a hint of tears
in Gabriel's voice as he appealed to Lars and the captain, peering through the bars of the corral gate. Long
shadows stretched from the cliffs to the west and
slanted under the trees. All afternoon Gabriel had
worked, coaxing, wheedling, trying every means he
could think of to cajole the colt into getting a taste of
the milk. But it was no use.

"Come eat your supper," Lars said to the boy. "You

can try him again this evening." Reluctantly, Gabriel
went with the men. But at twilight, after a supper of
trout that the captain had caught in the river, he
started back with a rolled blanket over his shoulder.

"You goin' to *live* with that colt?" the captain demanded.

"Don't aim to leave him there alone," Gabriel said.
He saw Lars and the captain grinning at each other
when he glanced back.

At the corral he went through the same discourag-
ing process. Flash would have none of the bottle. Yet
in the dusk he looked thinner and more forlorn than
ever. Gabriel had heard of wild things who had died
rather than be tamed. Weary, disheartened, he spread
his blanket in the corner of the corral and sat down.

"I'll just sit here till he gets used to me," he told
himself, picking up the bottle of milk. "If he comes
over and noses around, his supper'll be ready for
him."

The sky was aflame with sunset. Crows winged
their way home overhead. Songbirds twittered in the
leafy cottonwoods. The breeze from the river felt cool
on Gabriel's cheek.

He did not mean to sleep. He meant to watch the
colt for any sign of interest in the bottle of milk. But
his head began to nod, and his wiry brown hands
went slack. Gradually he settled himself into a more
comfortable position against the poles of the corral.

The cawing of the crows seemed far away. Gabriel slept.

A sharp tug at the bottle jerked him into wakefulness. He was startled, but he managed to catch himself before he made an abrupt motion. Flash was nuzzling at the bottle, exploring it with his lips. Breathless, Gabriel sat still, holding the bottle firmly. As the colt began to suck, he tipped it ever so gently so that milk filled the nipple.

As soon as Flash got a taste of the milk, he went after it with enthusiasm, his short tail twitching back and forth. When the bottle was empty he nosed it about, nickered softly, and then put his velvety nose against Gabriel's cheek. He turned away, then, shook himself, and lay down a few steps from the boy. With a contented sigh he stretched out to sleep.

A grin spread slowly across Gabriel's brown face. Then he wrapped his blanket around him against the chill night wind and curled down in a corner of the corral. A huge silver moon sailed above the trees, and the stars sparkled in the dark sky. Happy now, the boy was soon asleep.

As summer went on, Gabriel's life took on a new pattern. Instead of following Lars and the captain about their chores at the cabin — they didn't trap in the summer — he had a busy life of his own.

His first job was to find a place for Flash to live. The log barn near the cabin was a snug enough shelter, but it smelled of dust and old hay and sparrows.

"I'll help you clean it out," Lars offered. Gabriel flung the door and windows wide, and carried out the old hay and swept down the cobwebs. Then helped Lars carry in the hay they had cut near the river and left to dry in the sun.

The captain made a rope halter for the colt, and Gabriel spent hours getting him used to it, down in the corral. The work was hardly necessary. Since his first taste of milk, the colt seemed willing to follow Gabriel anywhere.

"He thinks you're his ma." The captain grinned. "Puts me in mind of one time in Kintucky —" and he was off on a long tale Gabriel suspected was half invention.

Through the window that night, Gabriel could hear Flash's soft stampings as he settled himself to sleep. "Good sounds," thought Gabriel, as he snuggled down on his straw mattress. Sounds he had dreamed of, on many a quiet night.

But the nights were short. No sooner did the light of dawn fill the sky than Flash was nickering for his morning bottle. He even learned to open the gate of the barn lot and come right to the cabin door. After breakfast, Gabriel was off to the McLain place.

Mrs. McLain had been right when she said there would be plenty of work. Sweat ran down Gabriel's back as he pulled weeds from the garden. He learned to split shakes for the roof of the new sheepshed Mac was building. He chopped wood and piled it in the woodshed until he was sure there was enough to last for a hundred winters. Mac said nothing if he did satisfactory work. But if he didn't, Gabriel heard about it soon enough.

"Wood's too big for the fireplace," he'd say shortly. "And ye've been rooting out the turnips along with the weeds."

Much as Gabriel would like to have snapped back, he held his tongue. Flash needed the milk. And he was fairly paid for his work, for Mrs. McLain saw to it that there was milk not only for the colt but for Gabriel to drink as well. She often gave him his noonday meal, too. Meat and potatoes, fresh peas from the garden, cake and pie and pudding were welcome changes from the captain's beans and sour dough. Gabriel's wiry arms and legs began to fill out, and he learned to laugh and joke with Jean and little Brian.

One day in late summer Gabriel showed Mrs. McLain and Jean the sunny hillsides where the best huckleberries grow. They made a picnic of it, taking their lunch.

"Not like our brambles at home — but very good!" Mrs. McLain declared, tasting the juicy purple berries. "I must make some jelly. It's a pity the sugar is so dear, and must be brought so far!"

Gabriel's Patience Rewarded

Brian sat in the middle of the patch, his fat hands and face slowly turning purple with the juice. Gabriel and Jean practiced imitating birdcalls as they picked, and just for fun they made up a signal system for calling to each other in the woods.

In the quiet afternoon, some distance away from the patch of berries where Mrs. McLain was picking, Gabriel found courage to speak to Jean about something that had worried him for a long time.

"Your father does not like me," he said. Jean went on picking berries, her face hidden by her blue checked sunbonnet. She was silent for so long that Gabriel thought she had not heard.

"I say, your father does not like me," he repeated. "Is there — something I do that makes him angry?"

"No — nothing you do," Jean said softly. "He is not angry with you."

"But he does not like me," the boy persisted. "Is it because I am part Indian?"

Jean was very still. When at last she answered, she spoke as if she had thought out her words carefully.

"Gabriel," she said, "my father crossed the plains once before we came out here. He and a friend of his came out as scouts along with a wagon train, riding ahead to find water holes and watch for Indians.

"One day about noon they saw wagons ahead of them. They thought it was strange that the wagons weren't moving in the middle of the day, and the ani-

63

mals were scattered over the prairie. When they came to the wagons, they found that the caravan had been attacked by Indians. All the men had been killed. There were no women or children at the wagons, alive or dead, so Father and his friend knew they must have been carried off by the Indians. They and some of the other men from their wagon train trailed them and helped rescue the women and children from the Indian camp. I think — I think he always remembers that when he thinks of Indians."

"But that was not here!" Gabriel said. "That was another tribe — not the Nez Percés, my people. They have always been friendly to the white people."

"That is what Lars and the captain told us, soon after we came here," Jean said. "They told us how the Nez Percés helped the explorers, Lewis and Clark, on their expedition many years ago, and how they promised to be the white man's friends. But Father doesn't change his mind easily. He began to give Lars and the captain the cold shoulder when they talked of the Indians as friends. I expect that's why they never came back."

"Why did your father come here, if he thought the Indians were so dangerous?" Gabriel asked.

"I think Father feels that as long as we stay away from the Indians — keep them at arm's length — we're pretty safe," said Jean, letting her bonnet drop back on her shoulders. "He remembers what happened to the missionaries. You know — Dr. and Mrs. Whitman, who came all the way from the East to tell the Indians about God. The Indians killed them, after they had spent years teaching and doctoring them! That was right here in the Oregon Territory, too!"

"But a few of the Cayuse tribe did that!" Gabriel burst out. "It happened when I was little, but I've heard Lars and the captain talk about it. Lots of the Indians got the measles, and they thought the doctor had given it to them. He tried to help them, but some died. Then one of the Cayuses pretended to go to the doctor for medicine, and killed him when he turned to get it from the shelf. Then they went wild, and killed or carried off the mission people."

"How horrible!" Jean exclaimed.

"But the Nez Percés were just as stirred up as the settlers!" Gabriel said. "Most of the Cayuses, even, turned against the ones who did the killing. It is not fair to blame *all* the Indians!"

"I know," Jean agreed with a sigh, "but try to tell Father that!"

"I would never have asked him for the milk, only Flash would have died without it," Gabriel said, his voice bitter. "And I have done my best to pay him for it."

"You have paid for it," Jean said. "If Father did not think you were paying for it, he would not let you have it, and you can depend on that!"

Small comfort that was, Gabriel thought. It rankled to feel the Scotsman holding against him something he could not help. But what could he do?

At least Mrs. McLain and Jean were his friends. And as he thought of the lonely life he had led before he had known them, he knew he had much to be thankful for.

And there was Flash — his own horse — growing stronger and more beautiful every day. The very thought of the colt was a delight.

-10-

GABRIEL FINDS OUT
ABOUT
HIS PARENTS

IT WAS, altogether, a wonderful summer. But all summers must end. The days grew short, the mornings nippy. The cottonwood leaves turned yellow and dropped to form a carpet around the cabin. The captain was gone on his long pack trip to Fort Walla Walla for supplies, and Gabriel found the cabin lonely with only Lars for company.

Flash had outgrown his need for milk, and Gabriel did not make his daily trip to the McLain ranch as he had in the summer. But he still went now and then to visit Jean and her mother and little Brian. Sometimes he took a string of trout or a wild duck. Often he brought back a basket of tarts or a loaf of fresh bread. The McLain cabin was an inviting place, smelling of newly washed clothes and things cooking.

On this late autumn day, as Gabriel approached the cabin with a plump salmon he had caught in the river, things were strangely quiet. Mac's saddle horse was tied at the gate, and Mac himself came out of the cabin door as Gabriel stepped onto the porch.

"Afternoon, Gabriel." The short greeting was all Gabriel expected. Mac's hostility had turned to grudging acceptance, but he seldom had anything to say beyond the briefest word. Gabriel still felt uneasy in his presence, and was relieved to see the big Scotsman mount his horse and ride away toward the foothills where the sheep were pastured.

"Come in, Gabriel. We're having school," Jean called from inside the cabin.

"Softly, Jean! You'll wake Brian!" her mother cautioned. "Why, Gabriel, what a fine big salmon! Mac's no fisherman, even if he had the time for it. You do bring us the makings for some grand meals!"

It seemed strange to see Jean at the table with pencil and paper, instead of being busy at gardening or washing dishes or hanging out clothes. Gabriel watched over her shoulder as she made orderly lines of writing.

"I shall be glad when more settlers come so that we can have a school," Mrs. McLain said. "In the meantime, Jean must not grow up ignorant. This will be her second winter out of school — she mustn't get too far behind. Let's see your writing, lass."

Gabriel liked to hear Jean's mother talk. There was a soft *burr-r-r* to her r's, and the Scotch expressions were new and strange to him. Now Mrs. McLain looked critically at Jean's neat rows of writing.

"You are doing better," she said at last. "We'll stop for today. Can you read or write at all, Gabriel?"

"Why — why, no," Gabriel said.

"Come here," said Jean. "I'll show you how to write your name. Then you can surprise Lars and the captain."

Carefully, she printed GABRIEL in large letters. "There," she said, handing him the pencil. "Now you try."

Awkwardly, the boy grasped the pencil. Hands that were clever with a fishhook were clumsy with pencil and paper. But at last he managed a readable copy of his name.

"There, you can write!" Jean laughed, brown braids bobbing. "Now what's your last name?"

The question struck Gabriel like a thunderbolt. "I — I don't know. I guess it's — I just don't know."

"You don't know? What a funny thing — not to know your own name!" Jean giggled. Gabriel felt his face grow hot.

"Now don't tease the lad," Mrs. McLain said. "Folks out in these wilds don't have much need for long names, and that's sure. Here, Gabriel — when you go

69

home, take this little pot of jam. And many thanks for the salmon."

Gabriel smiled at her. He had a very warm feeling for this motherly woman who always seemed to know how he felt. But he did not stay much longer, and he did not take the paper on which he had written GABRIEL.

Questions seethed in him as he walked back toward the home cabin in the pale golden sunlight. Who was he? What had happened to his father and mother? Questions, half-formed ever since the visit to the Nez Percé camp the summer before, now demanded to be answered. He remembered only Lars and the captain. No — there was someone else. A tall man who had carried him about on his shoulder. Gabriel remembered the excited half-afraid feeling of looking far down at the ground from his perch.

And there was someone else — or was she a dream? A woman with shining dark eyes and long dark hair. There was firelight somewhere in the dream, and a soft, gentle song. He hadn't thought of these things for a long time, but now his mind reached far back into the past, seeking answers to his questions.

As Gabriel came near the cabin he heard a familiar voice.

"The captain is back!" he said, half aloud, and hurried his steps. But before he reached the open door, the captain's words halted him.

"Half the money for the skins we got trappin' all last winter, I had to give for this grub!" he complained, as he stowed bags and bundles away on the shelf. "And pack it more'n a hundred miles, uphill and down, at that, besides hiring some Indians to canoe me across the river! I tell you, Lars, this is no life. They's other places we can go — and we'd better git, 'fore we grow fast to these blamed mountains!"

"There's other places," Lars agreed. "Places where we'd starve, maybe. Here, we got a roof over our heads and grub on the shelf. And there's the boy."

"Yes, there's the boy." That was all the captain said, then, for he looked around to see Gabriel standing in the doorway.

"Wood box is empty," said Lars. Gabriel went without a word to the woodpile.

At supper, Gabriel only half listened to the captain's story of his pack trip to the fort. How was he to find out what he needed to know? He should have asked Lars and the captain long before. But he remembered the evening they had told him he was part Nez Percé. Lars's tone, gentle though it was, had not invited questions. And the captain, he felt, might only laugh at him.

But now he must know. Late that evening, when Lars was yawning and the captain had finished his tale, Gabriel asked his question.

"Where did I come from?" There was a snort of mirth from the captain.

"Ha! Lars turned over a boulder, and there you was! Or maybe we found you in the shade of a sage-bush," the captain said, "or in a hollow stump, like a chipmunk." He grinned broadly at his own humor. He was still chuckling as he climbed into bed. Soon he was snoring, a half-smile on his bewhiskered face.

Gabriel did not smile. He felt his cheeks grow hot, remembering his embarrassment that afternoon at the McLains'.

Lars had said nothing. But now he tossed a fresh cottonwood knot on the dying fire and turned to Gabriel.

"I knew you'd be asking again, some day, who you were," he said. "You were too little to remember what happened to your ma and pa. And we never told you because — well, because we didn't think you were old enough to understand. Or maybe because the captain and me weren't brave enough." The blue eyes were kind and a little sad.

"I do have to know," Gabriel said. "I have to know what happened to my mother and father. I don't even know my last name!"

"Your pa was a man from the East," Lars said. "Martin Horne was his name. Tall fellow, fine-looking, educated-like. Came West around 1843, I recollect he said. He and your ma built this cabin, dug the well, built the barn, and fenced a pasture for their horses. The missions were still open then — that was before the massacre. Your ma had lived at the Lapwai Mission after her parents died, and your pa met her there. They looked for more settlers to move in, so they'd soon have neighbors.

"The captain and I came here one blustery day in the fall of 1848. We were on our way to Californy — they'd just found gold there, you know. Cap was sure we'd strike it rich there. We never meant to trap. Thought we'd some day get in on a gold strike. But we never did.

"Well, we weren't used to the country, and we didn't get out ahead of the weather. Then I got sick. The captain half carried me that last mile or two, after we sighted the smoke from the cabin. By the time we got here, I was more dead than alive. Don't even remember comin' in. Feverish, I guess." He stopped, remembering.

"I was sick for a long time," he went on. "Your ma took care of me. Then, when I got so I could travel, winter had set in for certain. You know how 'tis when the wind drifts the snow around the cabin and everything freezes up solid. So we stayed.

" 'Twas a bad winter. The snow was so deep all the deer had worked down the river to where they could find a little grass along the streams. Your family's supplies were running mighty low, what with having us two to feed. So along toward spring your pa decided to go on a hunting trip down the river — stay overnight maybe.

"Your ma wouldn't hear of his going alone, and finally he agreed that they'd both go, and the captain and me would stay with you. The snow was too deep for horses, but they had sure-footed Indian ponies, and they planned to pick their way close to the river where the snow wasn't so deep, and take their time. They had enough food to last two or three days; your pa knew the country, and how to keep warm, and your ma was as much at home outdoors as in.

"You were just a little feller, going on three years old. Little as you were, they used to take you on the horses sometimes. When they left that morning, with the sun shining and the trees all sparkly with frost, you thought you were going for a ride.

"But of course they couldn't take you on a trip like that. You were mighty disappointed when you found you couldn't go. But we coaxed you into drying your tears and waving them good-by before they were out of sight."

Lars stopped speaking. The knot in the wood snapped, sending a shower of sparks up the chimney. Gabriel gazed at the old trapper as he stared into the fire — the flowing beard, the broad, high forehead, the deep-set eyes. Lars was silent so long that Gabriel couldn't keep still.

"Did — they come back?" It was a question he had to ask, yet he felt he knew the answer. Lars turned to look at him.

"That's the part that makes me wish you hadn't asked about your pa and ma, Gabriel," he said. "But you ought to know.

"The good weather didn't last. By night the wind began to blow and it started to snow. The captain and me worried about your ma and pa, and hoped they'd found a good sheltered spot to make camp. In between times we talked about Californy and wished we were there, panning gold in the sunshine. That night you worried for your ma, and cried yourself to sleep."

"What was she like — my mother?" Gabriel whispered.

"She was a Nez Percé girl," said Lars. "Little slip of a thing, with big dark eyes and those long braids down her back. Running Deer, her Indian name was — she had an English name, too, but your pa liked her Indian name best. Her parents had died when she was little — eight or nine years old, maybe — and she'd lived at the mission.

"Pretty, she was. Mighty good to your pa — and to the captain and me, too. She used to sing you to sleep every night. A lullaby, sort of, though I could never tell whether it was a Nez Percé song or one she'd learned at the mission. That's why you missed her so, when your bedtime came."

Dark eyes — long dark hair — then it was not a dream, but a memory! Lars went on.

"The storm didn't let up that night or the next day. When your parents didn't get home at night that second day, the captain and me were really worried. But there was nothing we could do in the dark, with not so much as a burro to ride to go look for 'em.

"In the morning the storm had let up. I started out at daylight, but it wasn't until dusk that I found them. There had been a snowslide — the horses had lost their footing. They were all in the bottom of a canyon — the horses and your pa and ma — under an avalanche of snow and rocks. They were all dead."

Lars was silent. It was very quiet in the cabin, and dark but for the glow of the dying fire. Gabriel could not speak.

"That's about all there is to tell, Gabriel," Lars continued at last. "Except that the captain and me took care of you as best we could. We took up your pa's trap lines — he was trapping winters to get a little money ahead — and just carried on. We aim to see that you get the land your pa meant you to have. He looked forward to the day he could put in a claim for a homestead. He had great plans for a cattle ranch, with you to help him run it when you grew up.

"He was a fine man, your pa. No one ever thought more of his family than he did of you and your ma. You can be proud of him — and your mother, too."

Proud? But they were dead, gone before he'd ever had a chance to know them, Gabriel thought, to know what it was to have a mother and father! All he had was a misty memory.

It was too much to take in all at once. Lars, staring into the fire, was remembering something that had happened years before. But to Gabriel the tragedy was fresh and sharp. Silently, he slipped from the cabin.

Back of it, away from the river, rose the steep, rocky bluff with Gabriel's secret cave near the top. Hardly knowing where he was going, he climbed the path, not with his usual sense of adventure but with his heart full of an aching loneliness. Night surrounded him. A great white moon rode high over the canyons and touched with silver the winding river.

Last night Gabriel would have been afraid to come alone. But now the strangeness and the whisper of the wind echoed the loneliness in his heart. He strained to remember his parents — the tall man, the woman singing in the firelight. He felt as if he had found them, only to have them snatched away. The sense of loss was almost too much to bear.

Then from the corral below came a faint nicker — a soft, questioning call. For the first time since he'd had Flash, Gabriel had been so deep in his own thoughts that he had forgotten the colt. Now he slipped back down the trail.

Flash met him, his head barely reaching over the corral bars beside the barn. Gabriel was over in a second, his arm around the colt's neck, his hand gentle on the velvety nose. The colt was warm against his side.

He thought of the colt's mother, the black mare, dead at the bottom of a gully because she tried to rescue her baby. And he thought of his own mother and father, forever lost to him.

Standing there, the boy sensed a closeness that began to fill the empty place in his heart. He could not guess that in days to come his need of Flash would be even more desperate.

have forgotten the call of the wild ones. But would it always be so?

Today, in the mountains, Flash had suddenly pricked up his ears, snorted, and stared across a canyon at a far slope. Following his gaze, Gabriel had seen the band of wild horses grazing. Flash called to them, but they made no response. It was with difficulty that Gabriel turned him homeward. Even now, with the cabin and barn in sight, he was still nervous and spooky.

Suddenly Gabriel's eyes fixed on a tiny line of moving figures on the road far below. There were two men on horses. One horseman was leading a loaded pack mule.

"The captain's back!" Gabriel cried, aloud. "Let's go, Flash!" He touched the golden flanks with bare heels, and Flash was off, picking his way with sure feet among the sagebrush and clumps of buffalo grass.

As Gabriel rode, he could see the little group turn from the wagon track into the path that led to the cabin. This fall the captain had not made the long trip to Fort Walla Walla on foot. He had gone with young George Wright, on George's extra horse, and they had planned to bring back supplies for themselves and the McLains on George's mule. The trip down the river and across the mountains to the fort was new to George. He had welcomed the captain's company, and had been glad to have someone with him who knew how to talk to the Indians they would need to hire to ferry them and their goods across the river.

Now, Gabriel saw, they were back. He could hardly wait to hear about the captain's trip. Next year, he told himself, he and Flash would go, too! It had been the captain's idea, not his, that he stay home this year.

George had unloaded the captain's share of the provisions and was on his way up the valley by the time Gabriel reached the cabin. Gabriel could hear the captain talking as he came in the door.

"This is it, I tell you, Lars!" he was saying, "Gold — did you hear me — gold! No little line of dust, washed out with a dribble of water! This is *real* gold! They'll be comin' in by the dozens, stakin' claims every day! Ah — Gabriel! I wondered where you were, young'un! Did you hear — they've discovered gold! We'll be rich — all of us. We got to get there right away!"

The captain was pacing the floor. The cabin seemed too small to contain his excitement. His cap, more battered and grimy than ever, lay on the floor where he had pitched it. His round face was red, his forehead glistening with perspiration. Gabriel looked at Lars. There was a gleam of excitement in his eyes, too.

"Man by the name of Pierce discovered it," the captain went on. "It's on a creek, a little ways up off the Clearwater. The fort's a-buzzin' with the news." The captain sat down on the bench by the table.

"You know we've heard talk of gold up in the Nez Percé country for a couple or three years," he went on. "Indians wearin' gold ornaments and all that. But the treaty with the Indians kept anyone from prospectin' on the Clearwater.

"Then Captain John Mullan went in with a crew of men to build a road, way up there where no white men had been. When they came back, they really started the rumors flyin'! Then this Captain Pierce got friendly with the Nez Percés near where the mission used to be. Traded with 'em, and they took him on hunting trips, way up the Clearwater. It was there he saw certain signs o' gold.

"He didn't say anything, but he got some other fellers, and they went in — five of 'em. O' course, they got turned back by the Nez Percés, 'cause o' the treaty. But then they got next to old Chief Timothy's daughter — a right pretty young squaw, they say, named Jane — and she led 'em in a secret way to Canal Gulch, way up the river.

"Well, they prospected some, but didn't find anything at first. 'Twas after supper one night — 'twasn't more'n two or three weeks ago — one of 'em decided there was light enough to wash another pan or two before dark. Pretty soon the others heard him yell! *Gold!* He'd found it!

"Three cents' worth, they say, in that pan! Three cents' worth, young'un — but enough to start a gold rush!"

The captain stopped for breath. Lars was leaning forward, eyes ashine. Gabriel had never seen him look as he did now.

The provisions the captain had brought home were scattered about the cabin. He picked his way among bags and bundles as he paced the floor, full of his astonishing news. Dusk fell, and Gabriel lit the fire and put on the coffeepot. He found a couple of cold biscuits to eat — no one else seemed able to think of food.

"If we're going to get ready to go down there in the next day or so, 'pears we ought to get a little sleep," Lars said at last.

"By golly, I *am* tuckered, and that's a fact," the captain said. "These here vittles won't hurt 'til mornin', and then we'll have to see what we'll take with us. But here — I like to forgot somethin' important.

"You recollect Hank, o' course, and the fellers that captured the wild horses? I ran into him at the fort. He had a great tale o' woe about what bad luck they'd had. One o' the two-year-olds got away from 'em, and the other one was stole. I began to feel right sorry for 'im. Then the old man Lige came up and asked him did he pay me for the grub they ate while they were here. It came out, then, that they'd done right well with the two yearlings, and old Lige stood there while Hank counted me out what he figured they owed us. No great fortune — but more'n I ever expected to see from those fellers. So I brought you a present, young'un, to celebrate."

Gabriel didn't care to be called "young'un" now that he was taller than the captain. But this was no time to protest. He took the parcel the captain handed him. New breeches, he guessed. He needed them bad enough! He tore open the package. His black eyes grew big as he looked at the contents. He stared, wordlessly, at the captain.

"Hold 'em up, young'un, and let's see if they fit," the captain said, a broad grin on his face. Still without a word, Gabriel held up the clothes — a pair of leggings and a jacket of light tan buckskin, beautifully fringed and decorated with bright beads and porcupine quills sewn in intricate patterns.

"Moccasins, too, looks like," Lars said, and Gabriel drew out a pair of soft moccasins decorated to match the leggings and jacket.

"Got 'em from the Treaty Indians — the Nez Percés who've gone on the reservation," the captain explained. "We hired some of 'em to canoe us across the river."

The firelight danced on the designs of bright red and yellow and blue, and light danced in Gabriel's

86

eyes as he looked from the captain to Lars and back
again to the captain. And then, because he couldn't
think of anything else, he said something he at once
wished he had not.

"I wonder," he said softly, "what Jean will say?"

He could tell by the look on the captain's face that
it would be a long time before he would forget that
remark!

-12-

ORDERED OFF
McLAIN'S LAND

THE MOMENT Gabriel's eyes opened the next morning, he heard the captain's voice.

"I wonder what Jean'll say?" he mimicked, grinning. Gabriel, embarrassed, didn't answer. But he was too excited about the new buckskins to be angry. Lars didn't say much — just grinned at the captain's teasing. Both of them were eager to be ready to go north. The captain was all for leaving at once; Lars thought it would take a full day to get their gear ready.

"You all set to go, young'un?" the captain asked over his coffee.

"Go?" Gabriel said. "I aim to stay right here."

The captain's eyes widened.

"But there's gold up there — lots of it! People will be comin' in from as far east as St. Louis, from Canady,

88

up from Californy to stake out claims. We missed the Californy strike in '48 — but this time we'll get there first! Ain't you goin', too? You'll be rich!"

"Don't know what I'd do with a bunch of gold," Gabriel said.

"He don't know what he'd do with a bunch o' gold!" the captain repeated, turning to Lars. "Now I know it's true — that little Jeanie's gone to his head for sure!"

"Reckon you can get along here alone, should we go without you?" Lars asked.

" 'Course," Gabriel said. "I can get plenty of game, like I have been. I can trap, if I have to. I've stayed alone before, when you've been gone overnight on the trap lines. But I'll be lookin' for you back," he finished with a shy grin.

"That's to be seen," Lars said. "If we find all the gold the captain says is there, we'll be ridin' back on a solid gold mule!"

So Lars and the captain went about their preparations for their trip. Gabriel, after bringing in wood and water, feeding and brushing Flash, and taking a dip in the river, dressed in his new buckskins and mounted his horse.

"You'll not leave before morning?" he asked.

"Reckon not," Lars said. "We'll stay tonight and get off 'fore dawn tomorrow."

"I'll be back by sundown," Gabriel said. Then he

was off. Mounted on the dancing Flash and dressed in the beaded buckskins, he looked the very picture of a young Nez Percé brave.

At the touch of Gabriel's heel, Flash turned off the road onto the lane that angled across the meadows to the McLain ranch. He grinned to himself as he thought of what Jean would say when she saw him. Mrs. McLain always greeted him warmly, and Brian, now a chubby boy of four, openly worshiped him and lived for the day when his mother would let Gabriel take him for a ride on Flash.

But what about Mac? Gabriel had a brief surge of misgiving, recalling Mac's old hatred of Indians. He might not be so favorably impressed by this resplendent Nez Percé garb!

Still, Gabriel thought, he'd been going to the Mc-Lain ranch for three years. He'd worked for Mac all that first summer, and he'd often given him a hand when the work was heavy. Mac had even given him an occasional "Good job, lad" — lavish praise from the short-spoken Scot. Besides, there had been not a hint of trouble with Indians in the years the McLains had lived on the Salmon River. Surely Mac's distrust of them must be a thing of the past.

Anyway, it was Jean he was going to see. She could be a terrible tease when she felt like it, but she was always glad to see him.

Well, today she'd have something to see! He

touched Flash with his heels, and they swept up before the McLain cabin with a flourish. Brian stood in the doorway, a piece of bread and huckleberry jam in his hand. At sight of Gabriel he let out a whoop.

"O-o-o-h! Gabriel's all dressed up! Can't he take me for a ride on Flash today, Mother? Look, Jeanie, look at Gabriel's new suit!"

Jean's eyes widened when she came around the cabin. Her brown braids were turned under and tied with ribbon the same deep blue as her eyes.

"My, how fine we are!" she exclaimed. Gabriel couldn't tell if she was teasing. He swung off and dropped the reins to the ground. Flash moved a step and began cropping clover.

"You stay out of Flash's way, Brian," Jean said sharply. She never quite trusted the lively young stallion, though she rode well on her own little mare Blackbird or old brown Dolly that her mother sometimes rode. "Go wash your face and hands," she went on to her little brother. "You're sticky from your jampiece." The boy disappeared into the cabin.

"You look — real handsome, Gabriel," Jean said, not teasing this time. Now Gabriel was at a loss for words.

"The Captain brought it to me," he said, finally. "Guess he thought I needed some new clothes." Then he told Jean about the new gold strike, and Lars's and the captain's prospecting trip. Brian came back, slightly less sticky. Gabriel lifted him to let him pat Flash's soft nose.

There was a movement at the cabin door. Gabriel turned, expecting to greet Mrs. McLain. Instead Mac stood there, his face dark with anger.

"Put the boy down." Mac's voice was hard. Startled, Gabriel set Brian on the ground. "Go in the cabin, Brian. And you, Jean." Mac glared at them.

"But Papa — " Jean began.

"In the cabin!" Mac thundered, the dark color coming up under his tanned skin. He did not look like a man to argue with, with his broad shoulders and stubborn jaw. A lock of his black hair looked out of place falling over his forehead. His eyes, deep-set and blue like Jean's, could flash fire. Gabriel stared at him, bewildered.

Brian ran to Jean and took her hand, looking at his father with frightened wide eyes. She led the little boy into the cabin. Inside, Gabriel could see Mrs. McLain. Her hands were clasped so tight the knuckles showed white; he had never seen her look so upset. What had he done?

"I wasn't hurting Brian," Gabriel said.

"That's neither here nor there," Mac said. "You're to get out of here. Off this ranch. You and your Cayuse. You're never to come here again, or to touch one of my family. If I ever see you on this place again, I'll not be responsible for what happens. Now go!"

92

Gabriel stared, shocked. The cabin swam before him. He did not move.

"Go!" Mac thundered. Gabriel felt the hot blood rise in his face.

"Why?"

"For the same reason I ordered you off the first day you came here," Mac growled. "Because you're an Indian and a savage and not to be trusted. Because your kind murders women and children — murders the missionaries who come to help you. They killed the Whitmans at Waillatpu. And they're at it again. That's why! Now, go!"

Gabriel drew himself up to his full height — not much less than Mac's own. His face was like a rock. But the black eyes were blazing.

"For hundreds of years my mother's people lived in this land," he said. "Then the white men came. Some came to find homes; some came to get rich. Some of them live at peace with the Indians. But some fence the land, kill the wild things, push the Indians back and back from the good land. I know how the Indians have been pushed onto reservations.

"Now you order me from the land you call yours, because I was born in my mother's country, and my skin is a different color from yours." His level gaze did not waver as he looked into the Scotsman's eyes. Beyond Mac, in the cabin, stood Jean, white-faced, with her mother and little Brian. None of them spoke.

93

"I go," Gabriel said. He sprang onto Flash's back. A touch of his heels — and the horse was off, out of the yard, past the log barn, down the lane that led to the main road.

He did not look back.

–13–

WARNING OF INDIAN UPRISING

ONCE ON THE MAIN ROAD, Gabriel let Flash choose his pace. The boy's mind was in turmoil. A kingfisher perched on a bare snag above the river's edge, and a chipmunk scolded from a yellow pine near the road. But Gabriel saw neither bird nor animal. He was burning with anger.

What had Mac called the Indians — murderers, savages? Gabriel had heard talk about trouble between the Indians and whites from Hank and his men. From others, too. Visitors did not come often to the cabin, but an occasional trapper like Pierre would stop now and then, and news would be relayed.

Strange man — Pierre. Solitary, like most of the trappers, but having even less to say than most of those who stopped for a cup of coffee and a plate of

95

beans with Lars and the captain. He was a French Canadian — dark-skinned, unsmiling, his long hair caught in a sort of queue at the back of his head.

Once when he had come, Pierre had told of the Nez Percés in the Wallowa Mountains. Their leader, Old Chief Joseph, had refused to sign the treaty that would give the white men the right to settle in the valley that was their home — the Valley of Winding Waters. Gabriel had listened silently, hardly realizing that the distinction between white skin and brown would some day be vital to himself.

Now Mac's words had brought it home to him. Hot anger mingled with bitterness and humiliation. He was not a savage, a murderer, because other Indians had killed the missionaries! Had not his mother and father taken in Lars and the captain, who where white men, when they were in trouble? True, Indians had killed women and children and settlers who were doing them no harm. But were they to move back without a word until the land was gone, the deer and waterfowl killed, the rivers polluted? Indian women and children had been killed, too — who was to speak for them?

Flash started to turn into the lane leading home, but Gabriel reined him the other way. Go in and tell the captain and Lars that Mac had ordered him off his ranch? He couldn't! He turned Flash toward the jack pine grove where he had been the first day he'd seen the horses. Here, while Flash cropped grass on a shaded slope in the warm afternoon, Gabriel lay on the pine needles and brooded.

He could still see Mrs. McLain's clenched hands, Jean's stricken eyes. Jean's one feeble word had been silenced by her father. Gabriel had half expected Mrs. McLain to come to his defense. She had always been his friend — had given him milk for Flash, had welcomed him into her homey cabin, had even helped him learn to read and write. But today she had said nothing. Fresh anger welled up in him. Then came the idea.

He would go with Lars and the captain! Gold, they had said! They would be rich when they staked their claim in the new gold fields! Well, he would go with them, and he would be rich too. How blind he had been, to think he wanted to stay among these sun-blasted hills!

Excited now, he leaped to Flash's back. The sun was low — shadows stretched from the western ridges across the bottom lands. The cabin lay in shadow. Strange, thought Gabriel, as he slid from the horse's back in front of the door, that no smoke rose from the chimney, no firelight glowed through the window. The captain should be getting supper now, so that he and Lars could get a good night's sleep and an early start in the morning. Gabriel flung open the door.

The cabin was filled with the gloom of evening. It had the feeling of a house left empty.

"Lars! Captain!" the boy called. There was no answer. He crossed to the fireplace, poked at the ashes until he uncovered a spark. Some dry chips, a bigger stick or two, and light danced on the smoky rafters, the hanging bags of beans and rice.

Then Gabriel saw the note on the table. It was in Lars's careful hand. It read:

Gabriel: The captain and me caught a ride down the river with some new people looking for a place to settle. The chance was too good to miss. Take care of yourself.

LARS

Gabriel read the note in the flickering firelight. It was hard to believe that Lars and the captain were really gone.

Of course, he'd known they were going — had expected them to leave in the morning. He'd made it plain enough that he could get along without them, that he didn't intend to go with them. But that was this morning. Now he felt outcast, lonely, deserted.

Gabriel held the note to the brightening light of the burning wood and slowly read it once more. Then he crumpled it into a ball and pitched it into the fireplace.

The cabin was a forlorn place in which to live alone. In the days that followed, Gabriel spent as much time away from it as he could. He shot enough game and caught enough fish to live on, along with biscuits and coffee, but it didn't take much time to do that. He explored canyons and streams he'd never seen before. One afternoon, for lack of anything better to do, he even picked a mess of late huckleberries on a shaded north slope.

Back at the cabin, he dawdled, feeding Flash and rubbing him down. At last there was nothing else to do but go in and get his supper. Biscuits from the Dutch oven, a couple of trout broiled over the coals, a bowl of huckleberries — it was soon on the table. Gabriel turned to pour the coffee into the tin cup.

"Ye home?"

Gabriel jumped, and came near to dropping the pot. He turned to see the trapper Pierre outlined in the doorway against the dark red of the sunset sky. His face brightened with a smile of welcome.

"Come in! Sit down. I'll get a cup and plate!"

The old trapper was dressed in a grimy wool shirt and worn homespun breeches, his hair in the usual queue under his greasy felt hat. His thin and weather-beaten face was empty of expression. But to Gabriel no guest had ever been so welcome.

"Where's Lars and the captain?" asked Pierre, ignoring Gabriel's invitation. The boy told him of the newly discovered gold and of the men's hasty leaving. Pierre showed no surprise.

"I come to warn ye," he said solemnly.

"Warn me? Of what?"

"Trouble. Indian trouble. Indians don't like white men muddying up their streams, gouging into their Mother Earth. Up to now the Treaty Indians have been quiet. But now they've found gold, the whites are coming in — lots of them. Onto the reservation. And the Indians are stirred up.

"Not the old chiefs. Not the Nez Percés. Young bucks, stragglers from the Cayuse. Young bucks with whisky, eager for trouble."

Gabriel stared at the trapper, the food forgotten.

"Last night they burned a cabin, down the river," Pierre went on. "Man and wife just got away with their lives. The Cayuses are comin' this way — five of them, on horses. No telling what they'll do. May sleep it off, sober up, go home. May get more whisky, burn more cabins. I come to warn ye. Ye'd better be on the lookout."

"But we've had no trouble," Gabriel said. "The only Indians we ever see are the Nez Percés who go up into the valley to fish and hunt, and go to their Council Mountain in the fall, way to the south. Lars and the captain were always friendly with them."

"Makes no difference. Some white men hate all Indians. Some Indians hate all white men. Whisky takes away what little sense they might have. Pays to keep a sharp watch — and not be in the cabin when they come."

"What about Lars and the captain?" Gabriel asked.

"They speak the Indian tongue — they can talk to the Cayuses if they have to," Pierre said. "They're armed — and they're not alone. They'll be safe."

"And what about you?"

Pierre shrugged, and for the first time a hint of a smile played around his mouth.

"No Indian knows this country like Pierre. Ask the beaver. You know the country, too. You've got a good horse. Just stay out of their way. But you'd best warn your friends up the valley — the Scotsman with the sheep."

A black shadow passed over Gabriel's face. "They are not my friends," he said. A grizzled eyebrow shot up, querying. That shrug again.

"As you say. But Indians are more apt to make trouble for those who fence their land and put it to the plow than for those who hunt and trap and fish. And there's a woman and children."

"They've a man to look after them," Gabriel said sullenly. They ate then, hastily and with few words.

Soon Pierre stood at the door. Gabriel tried to thank him for the warning.

"Lars and the captain always my friends. Always coffee, food, warm fire. You my friend, too."

He was gone then. Gabriel watched him go down the path from the cabin, a shadow among the shadows cast by a three-quarter moon in a buttermilk sky. For a moment he looked back at the fire. When he turned again to watch Pierre, the old trapper had vanished.

A DIFFICULT DECISION

Back by the fire, Gabriel found it hard to believe that Pierre had really been there with his disturbing news. It was strange — for these last weeks, ever since Mac had sent him off his ranch because he was an Indian, Gabriel had thought of himself as one of them. Now he had been warned against the Indians. Fear for his own safety did not trouble him. But there was a gnawing question at the back of his mind. Whose side was he on? And what about the McLains?

"They are not my friends," he had told Pierre. He would let it go at that. Mac could take care of his wife and Jean and little Brian, Gabriel told himself. Had he not ordered him away and as much as threatened him with his life if he should return? Then why should he trouble to warn them?

103

Gabriel had made up his mind. He would take his bedroll and a little food, and spend the night in his secret cave behind the cabin. The path was too steep for Flash, but he could lead the horse around by another way to a broad grassy slope in sight of the cave, and picket him there for the night. If the Cayuses should come to the cabin at all, they would conclude it was unoccupied.

It was exciting, thinking of himself and Flash — his one remaining friend — hiding out through the night. He kicked the embers apart and let the fire die. He made a bundle of the leftovers of supper, added some dried venison, and rolled up a couple of blankets for a bed.

Flash came to the corral bars at his whistle. Because the barn was snug and warm in the winter, but airless on the hot evenings of summer and fall, Gabriel left Flash outside until the nights began to get nippy. Flash's blaze shone white in the moonlight, and his light creamy mane feathered out in the night breeze. The boy thrilled to the feel of the velvet nose, the firm silky neck.

"Just you and me, Flash," he said softly. The horse threw up his head, his ears cocked forward. He paced restlessly around the corral, tail swishing, then came back to Gabriel. Once more fear came into the boy's heart. What would happen if Flash heard the wild horses near, and the call became too strong to resist?

A *Difficult Decision*

The corral fence was high. But what if Flash should remember his old trick of opening the gate he had learned when he was little? That was long ago — now there was a new and stronger gate on the corral. Still, how could he be sure Flash would not find a way to get out if he really wanted to?

But there was no time to worry now. Gabriel picked up his bedroll and food from where he had dropped them by the corral gate, and started up the trail.

It took longer to climb to the cave than it had when he had scrambled up empty-handed. Near the top he dropped the bedroll, and it went tumbling to the foot of the steep trail. But at last blankets and food were stowed in the cave.

Now to bring Flash the long way around, up a winding and less steep trail. Gabriel started down, but at the head of the trail he paused, his gaze sweeping the shadowy landscape of broken canyons and winding river. Far to the south, through the dark shadow that would be the cottonwood grove, he saw a light — a pinprick in the lonely darkness. The McLain's light.

Gabriel had seen it before, when he had come here at night. A friendly light it had been then. But now he turned from it, his jaw set.

He looked north, where the river began to hurry its course, bursting to foam as it tumbled over the rocks. Across the river to the west lay the rugged Seven Devils, already snow-capped, ghostly in the moonlight. His gaze swept south once more, drawn to that point of light.

The McLains had had no warning, that was sure, for if they suspected trouble from the Indians they would never have let a light show to point out their cabin. But their safety was Mac's affair, Gabriel told himself. Let him take care of them. He thought of Mrs. McLain, whose good scones and pies and roast chicken he had eaten, who had given him milk for Flash, who seemed to understand him, sometimes, better than he understood himself. Little Brian, always begging for a ride. Jean — changeable Jean, teasing, scolding, laughing. He was an Indian — and because he was an Indian he had been ordered away from their home. And none of them had said a word in protest.

An Indian? He would be one of them, then! Others had joined the tribes — why not he? He remembered the Nez Percés who camped along the river, and how they had welcomed him and Lars and the captain to their fireside. He thought of them now with longing.

But what if he fell in with a tribe who expected him to go with them on such a raid as Pierre had told him about? Would he join them in setting fire to cabins, killing settlers? Never!

Yet who was right? Should not the Indians resist

those who came to take their land? Gabriel turned over the question in his mind as if he were the first young man to try to separate the wrong things in the world from the right, as if on his shoulders alone rested the problems of the white man and the red.

Then, suddenly, it came to him — *he* did not have to judge between his mother's people and his father's! There were fair and honest white men — there were kind and friendly Indians. And there were those, both white and red, who were cruel and wicked. His choice was not between white and Indian, but between right and wrong!

It was like the sun rising. Gabriel saw things clearly now. One thing he knew — it was wrong to drive people from their homes. One thing he could do — he could warn the McLains. It would not take long to get there, riding Flash. Then it would be up to Mac to find his family a safe place until the danger was past.

He started down the trail, quickly now, sliding a little at the steep turns. Across the little open space toward the barn, whistling softly as he went. Flash would be at the gate, waiting for him.

The gate? The gate was wide open! The corral was empty.

-15-

WARNING THE McLAINS OF DANGER

Stunned, Gabriel stared at the empty corral. Flash couldn't have left the corral in the little time he'd been at the cave! Or could he?

"I would have seen him go!" Gabriel said to himself. But would he? The cabin could be seen from the head of the trail. But the barn and corral, tucked away in the shelter of the bluff, would have been out of sight.

"He got out while I was gone!" Gabriel whispered, hardly able to believe it himself.

Still, Flash could not have gone far. Gabriel whistled, the low whistle that always brought Flash to him.

The night wind rustled the cottonwood leaves. Crickets chirped in the dry grass. That was all.

But Flash *couldn't* be far away! Perhaps he was nosing around the cabin, remembering his baby days. Or browsing somewhere near. With mounting anxiety, Gabriel circled the cabin, whistling, listening, whistling again.

Could he possibly have put Flash in the barn and forgotten he had done so? He knew he hadn't. Yet he went to the empty corral, peering into every corner as he crossed it, and opened the barn door. Whistle again — of course Flash wasn't there! There was only the pungent smell of wild hay — and empty darkness.

Once more around the cabin, straining his eyes up and down the riverbank as he went. Nothing.

So it happened, the thing he had feared. The call of the wild band had been too much for Flash. For the first time since the leggy colt had taken his milk from the bottle in Gabriel's hands, the boy felt completely alone.

Lars and the captain were gone. His friends the McLains had rejected him. And now Flash, his dream horse, his companion, had deserted him. And what of the trapper's warning? How was he to alert the McLains without Flash?

He could walk, of course. Yes, that was what he must do. It was as if he had never had Flash.

Would the sorrel stallion ever come back? Perhaps he would find him, Gabriel thought, as he gazed toward the shadowy ridges. On some upland meadow he would call, and Flash would look up, ears cocked, nostrils flaring. Then he would come to him, and Gabriel would slide his hand under the silky mane, and pat the velvet nose, and Flash would forget the wild horses.

But that was only a dream. How could he expect a horse who had once tasted the freedom of the mesas to be content in a corral? Oh, he would look for Flash. He would search every canyon, every upland pasture. But not unless the stallion came to him willingly would he try to catch him.

Now he had a job to do. The moon was high — it must be near midnight. The wind was blowing the curdled clouds apart. Between them distant stars floated in the clear deep blue.

Along the path from the cabin to the road Gabriel walked quickly, his moccasined feet making no sound. He planned what he would say to the Mc-Lains. His words would be few — he would just repeat what Pierre had told him. Then it would be up to Mac to protect his family. As for Gabriel, he would come back to his secret cave. In the morning he would look for Flash.

Until now, it had not occurred to Gabriel to be afraid of the Cayuses. Actually, he didn't think they would come. But what if they really *were* on their way up the canyon? What if they found *him*? In the strangeness of the night, with the moon casting misty shadows and an owl hooting mournfully from a distant pine, Gabriel found himself shivering.

He left the road and moved along near the river, keeping as much as possible in the shadows of willow clumps. Sometimes he dropped into the river bed, bare in spots now that the water was low, and traveled along the gravel bars in the shelter of cut banks or stands of cattails. There he stood a good chance of escaping the notice of anyone passing.

Of course, the Cayuses might not follow the road. But in the narrow canyon they would have to use it at least part of the way — and it had been an Indian trail long before it had seen a wagon wheel.

Up the river bed, silently and in haste. What was that? The tlot-tlot-tlot of horses' hoofs! Heart in mouth, Gabriel paused in the shadow of a big thornbush. He listened, holding his breath.

Nearer came the sound, and nearer. Muffled a little by the dry dust, but unmistakable. He strained to see the road. But the wild grass was tall and the road was above him, though only steps away.

Tlot-tlot-tlot! Down the dirt road — from the direction of the McLains'! Indians? Who else would be out at this hour but the Cayuses?

Breathless in his hiding place, his heart hammering in his ears, Gabriel waited. For a better view, he braced his foot against a twisted root, pulling himself up into the bush and clinging to the rough branches as he peered down the road. At that moment the horse came into view, a dark shape against the sky.

A single horse, riderless. For a moment he stood out against a bright cloud. Only for a moment. But in that instant Gabriel saw enough to set his heart racing.

Flash!

The marauding Cayuses were forgotten. Gabriel scrambled up to the road, whistling to Flash. Would he come? Gabriel held his breath.

Flash slowed, turned, and waited, head up, ears cocked. Gabriel whistled again. Flash's soft nicker was like music.

"Here, Flash!" Gabriel called softly. The horse nickered again, a wordless question. Then his nose was rubbing against the boy's shoulder. Gabriel's hand trembled as he ran it up behind Flash's ears and along his silky neck.

Then his hand met something rough and hard. He looked under Flash's mane.

A rawhide rope encircled the horse's neck. The broken end, hanging loose, told the story.

"The Cayuses!" Gabriel gasped. "They stole you! You didn't run away! They took you while I was at the cave!

"But you broke loose from them. You were free —
you could have gone with the wild horses — but you
came back to me!"

Then the horrible truth burst upon Gabriel. Flash
had been coming home — from the south, the direction of the McLain ranch! That meant but one thing
— the Cayuses were on their way there — or were
there already! In a second he had sprung on Flash's
back and turned the horse southward.

Then he stopped to think a moment. Flash might
have broken loose from the Indians only a short time
before. It was senseless to go dashing up the road,
perhaps at their very heels. He listened, breathless,
sorting out the sounds.

A lone cricket. Wind in the tall grass. The call of a
screech owl, which was not a screech but a tremu-
lous quaver.

And horses' hoofs. At first he thought it was imag-
ination. But as he listened the sound grew clearer —
not closer, just clearer because he was listening so
intently. Several horses, he judged, moving at a trot.
Voices? He couldn't be sure.

One thing *was* sure. Whoever the riders were, they
were much closer to the McLain cabin than he was.
But the lane to the cabin turned off the main road at
an angle, and meandered across the low-lying
meadow for almost a mile before it reached the

cabin. If he cut straight across to the cabin, he might, with speed and luck, reach it before the riders.

He turned Flash off the road, away from the river. With only the piece of broken rawhide to serve as a bridle, he was glad that Flash had learned to be guided by his voice and the movements of his body. If he could only get to the McLain cabin before the Cayuses! He didn't think beyond that.

Flash was crossing low ground, flat river meadows cut through here and there with the beds of mountain streams. One of the largest was Phantom Creek, which, having dashed and foamed down Phantom Canyon, now wound across the swale before emptying itself into the Little Salmon. Swamp grass, tall and coarse, masked dips and hollows. But the soft ground underfoot made Flash's hoofbeats almost noiseless.

Gabriel urged the horse on as fast as he dared over the uneven ground. There was no time to listen for the other horses. He must expect the worst.

Soon the grove of cottonwoods around the McLain cabin loomed as a dark shadow ahead, with the log barn another shadow a little beyond. The ground was rising now, toward the lowest foothills. With a word and a flick of his heels, Gabriel urged Flash on. As they neared the back of the cabin he drew up, and sat his horse, listening.

Horses! Walking now. Not half a mile away. He strained his eyes toward the road, but bushes and the cottonwoods were in his way. He could see nothing.

The cabin was dark. He slipped noiselessly from Flash's back and approached the window — the only door was in front — and rapped sharply. There was no sound. He hammered again.

"Mrs. McLain! Mac!" His whisper sounded loud in his ears. But there was no response. He tried once more. Still silence.

Were they all gone? Had someone already warned them of trouble? Gabriel stood, undecided. Then, inside, he heard a child sneeze. Brian!

"Mr. McLain! You're in danger! The Cayuses are coming!" Gabriel felt sure the approaching Indians would hear him. Then the window opened stealthily.

"Who is it?"

It was not Mac's voice. It was Mrs. McLain's. Her face was white in the dim light.

"Me — Gabriel! Tell Mac the Cayuses are coming!"

"Mac's not here! He left this afternoon to go to George Wright's. He should have been back long ago. Something's happened to him! Whatever can we do?"

Jean's frightened face appeared beside her moth-

116

er's. Brian climbed to the window. He was bursting with questions, but Jean hushed him to silence. Gabriel was thinking fast.

Mac not there? Then they were defenseless. It was up to him to find a way of escape!

16

SHADOW OF
THE
CAYUSES

"Listen!" Gabriel whispered. They stopped breathing. They could hear, faintly, horses splashing through water. That would be at the little stream that crossed the lane, perhaps a quarter of a mile from the cabin.

"You must get out of the cabin!" Gabriel whispered urgently. "They'll break in. You won't have a chance if you stay. What horses are here?"

"Dolly and Blackbird." Mrs. McLain's voice was tense. "They're in the barn."

"Get dressed. Don't light a candle. I'll saddle the horses and come back for you."

"But what about Mac?"

"He always carries a gun. He can take care of himself. But you must get out of the cabin!"

Jean was already dressing Brian, moving cautiously in the darkness, her voice the smallest whisper. Gabriel turned toward the barn, leading Flash. He knew where there was an extra bridle. An old one, but better than nothing. He'd use it for Flash.

He stopped to listen before he led the horses from the barn. No sound from the cabin. He swung back the door silently, leading Jean's little black mare and the brown pony Mrs. McLain rode. Still no sound from the cabin. No sound of horse's hoofs in the lane beyond. Gabriel slipped the bridle on Flash and started for the cabin. The horses were restless. Every sound of hoof on gravel made Gabriel cringe. His heart was racing, yet his mind was clear. He knew what they must do.

They must get away from the cabin unseen. They must cross the meadows, the way he had come, keeping under cover. Then they would follow the river until they reached his cabin. But they would not stay there — wouldn't even go in. They would climb to the secret cave, where they could hide in safety.

Back at the cabin, Mrs. McLain was at the window. Gabriel took Brian from her, then helped her to the ground. Jean dropped lightly to her feet and took Blackbird's reins from Gabriel. In a moment she was in the saddle.

Quickly Gabriel whispered his plan. Mrs. McLain nodded, and climbed on Dolly in grim silence.

119

"I'll take Brian," she said.

"He can ride with me," said Gabriel. Even in the near-darkness he could see the little boy's eyes shine with delight.

"Can you manage him on Flash?"

"He'll be safe," Gabriel promised. He swung Brian up. "Hold onto his mane," he said, as the boy's hand clung to his.

At that moment there broke out from the front of the cabin a blood-chilling shriek — the cry of the Cayuses! Mrs. McLain and Jean sat frozen with terror. But not Gabriel.

"Quick!" he whispered. "Stay close to us!"

He wheeled Flash, who was snorting with excitement. Blackbird and Dolly were at the sorrel's heels. Gabriel, riding with one arm around Brian, could feel the little boy's heart pounding against his ribs.

Down across the sloping meadow, angling toward the river. Keeping to the cover of banks and willows. Watching for hidden holes and grass-grown banks that could make a horse lose his footing. Looking back to see that Mrs. McLain and Jean were close behind him. And all the time, the yells of the Cayuses filling his ears.

The moon hung low in the west now, dipping toward the Seven Devils. The sky was clear, the stars luminous. Here and there along the river, wisps of mist moved before the fitful predawn wind.

What would the Cayuses do, there at the cabin? Gabriel wondered only briefly. Burn it? Perhaps. Better not think of that — he must use his wits to make sure they escaped unseen.

The noise from the cabin was fainter as they moved across the swale. No doubt the Indians were trying to frighten the settlers they supposed were in the cabin into showing themselves. Then the sound grew louder. In a hurried glance over his shoulder, Gabriel thought he could see dark shapes circling the cabin.

He kept Flash at a steady trot, not too fast because of the uneven ground. They had put a mile between them and the cabin, maybe more. Another mile, and they would be at the river. There the steep cut banks of the almost-dry bed would give more cover.

The moon was still bright. It cast long shadows of their moving forms across the broken ground. Try as he would to keep out of sight, Gabriel found many open spaces that had to be crossed. It made him shudder to think how clearly they might be seen by a sharp-eyed Cayuse looking in the right direction.

"Gabriel! They're coming!" Jean's voice was sharp with terror. He looked back. Out from the cottonwood grove moved a rider. Another, in a different direction.

They had not found the trail — yet. They must get to the river! Gabriel touched Flash with his heels.

"Hurry!" he called back. Blackbird was not a length behind. Even Dolly spurted forward. No time to lose now, even though they risked being seen. The Cayuses would soon pick up their trail. But perhaps they could throw the Indians off when they reached the gravelly river bed.

Flash was acting strangely. Gabriel had been too busy looking ahead to notice it at first. But now he was certain that Flash was pulling to the right, away from the river, toward the rocky foothills.

Gabriel pulled the stallion sharply to the left. Flash responded for a moment. Then he was fighting the reins as before. Strange — until now Gabriel had been able to guide him with the slightest touch against his neck.

Far behind, they heard a shriek. Gabriel glanced over his shoulder. The Cayuses! Riding at a gallop now, toward them. One in the lead, on a wiry spotted pony. Three more — no, four — behind him!

Gabriel touched Flash with moccasined heels. There was no need — the sorrel shot forward. Behind him, Blackbird and Dolly put on a new burst of speed. Close to his chest, Gabriel could feel little Brian breathing fast with excitement and half-understood fear. Gabriel pulled more sharply at the reins, urging Flash toward the river. It did no good.

Little by little, control passed from the boy to the horse. Flash dropped back a little now, abreast of the mares. He crowded them toward the foothills.

"Where are you taking us?" gasped Mrs. McLain. "I thought we were to make for the river!"

"Follow Flash!" Gabriel shouted. He did not understand what the big sorrel was doing — but somehow he felt that Flash did.

Gabriel's words were lost in the sound of rushing air and running hoofs. There was nothing he could do. Flash was out of his control. The stallion was running at the full speed of the mares, and he was pushing them toward the foothills. Behind them, the yells of the Cayuses rang in the air.

They struck Phantom Creek were it tumbled down the last steep grade from the mountains. Flash turned sharply up the canyon. The mares knew their leader. They followed only a length behind.

There was a trail, at first, wide enough for two horses abreast. But as they climbed, the canyon narrowed, the walls grew steep and rocky. Beside the trail Phantom Creek tumbled over rapids and falls. As the trail twisted, the high walls cut off the light of the moon. Only here and there it slanted down, softened by the growth of ferns and bushes on the rocky ledges.

"We shall all be killed!" Gabriel heard Mrs. Mc-Lain cry. He did not try to answer. It was all he could do to stay on Flash and hold Brian as they climbed the steep trail.

Around a bend, leaning with the horse's movement. Up a steep slope, bending forward. Catching his breath when they reached a few yards of level ground. Holding tight to Brian with one arm. Glancing back at the others. Watching — watching back at each bend for a Cayuse on a spotted pony.

There was one hope — only one. If by lucky chance the Cayuses had not seen them turn up the canyon, the Indians might waste some time finding the trail. If they could get out of the canyon onto the high tablelands beyond, they might find a way to elude their pursuers. Gabriel clung to the hope.

But not for long. Once more he heard the cries of the Cayuses, now echoing meanacingly along the canyon walls.

Suddenly Flash slowed, let the mares run past him at a wider spot in the trail. Then on, fast, at Blackbird's heels.

At their backs, as they rounded a curve, the low moon slanted, throwing great distorted shadows of horses and riders ahead of them against the high canyon wall.

Gabriel watched as the shadow horses rounded the

curve — Dolly with Mrs. McLain, Jean on Blackbird, himself and Brian on Flash. They disappeared, one by one, as they rounded the bend and passed out of the moonlight.

But behind them, Gabriel saw another shadow — the shadow of the Cayuse on the painted pony!

17

CANYON REFUGE

Flash spurted forward, crowding the panting mares. Then, as they rounded the next curve, he pushed past them. He slowed, ears forward, nostrils quivering.

The sound of rushing water filled the air. Then, unexpectedly, he turned, gathered his feet under him, and leaped the stream! The move was so sudden that Gabriel had to scramble to keep his seat, clutching Brian. Why, they were leaping straight into the canyon wall!

Cold spray was in Gabriel's face, and the slap of a wet hemlock branch. He glanced back to see first Dolly and then Blackbird leap the stream, following Flash.

The horses swung in a half circle, slowed, and stopped, panting, broadside to the trail.

"Why are we stopped?" Brian asked.

"Hush!" Gabriel whispered. He turned to Jean and her mother and waved a hand toward the trail. "Look — we're screened by the waterfall and those hemlocks. Keep still — they won't see us!"

They were in the deep shadow of an overhanging cliff, over which poured the waterfall. Through lacy boughs of mountain hemlocks and the silvery spray from the falls, they could barely see the trail.

Once more the yells of the Cayuses filled the canyon. Nearer came the sound, and nearer, mingled with the clatter of hoofs on the rocky trail. Gabriel could see him now, through the boughs — the Cayuse on the spotted horse. Would he follow their trail across the stream? The Indian came at the pinto's full speed up the trail. He did not pause! He was going on! He was waving his arm, yelling exultantly. He was sure he had almost caught up with his quarry — he thought they were still on the trail ahead!

Gabriel listened, breathless, as the hoofbeats grew fainter, the yelling died away. But that was only the first. In a moment they heard more hoofbeats, more yells. The rest of the Cayuses were close together, following their leader. They flashed by as flickers of movement through the boughs. Two almost together, then another, then one more. That should be all! Gabriel breathed a sigh of relief as the last hoofbeat died away along the trail.

"Will they come back?" Mrs. McLain's voice was almost a whisper. Gabriel shook his head.

"Who can tell? But we are safe now, for a little while, and we can rest the horses. And look — it's almost daylight."

The sky above the cliff was pearly, tinged faintly with pink. In the pale light they could make out their surroundings. They were in a little glade, shadowed on the east by the cliff over which the falls poured, and facing the steep rocky hillside.

The mares, still breathing hard, stood quietly. Flash, though his coat was salt-coated and covered with dust, was dancing with life, now that he had caught his breath.

Gabriel dropped to the ground and swung Brian down.

"Get off and rest, Mrs. McLain," he said. "And you, Jean." They tied the horses farther back in the clearing, so that they were completely screened from the trail by the hemlocks and the growth of fern and brush around the waterfall. Mrs. McLain sat down gratefully with little Brian in her lap.

"It's good to rest," she said, still breathless. "But now it's Mac I'm worried about. Whatever has become of him?"

"Perhaps he decided to stay overnight at George Wright's," Jean suggested.

"Oh no, Jeannie, he'd never do that — not with this

128

fright about the Indian uprising! He'd have come back if he could!"

"Then you'd heard about the Cayuses burning a cabin the night before last?" Gabriel asked.

"No — we heard nothing of that! It was — oh, ten days or more ago that George came to tell us there was trouble down near the reservation, where they've found gold. He said they didn't expect trouble this far south, but he wanted us to be on the alert.

"Of course we were on edge, especially Mac. He went about muttering to himself that he wished he'd never left Scotland. Then the very next morning you came galloping up, dressed in your Indian finery and looking as if you owned the world!

" 'He's joined the redskins!' Mac said, when he looked out and saw you ride up to the gate. 'He knows the cabin, the horses, all about us. He'll lead the savages right to us!'

"I could not talk him out of it. And the mood the man was in, I knew it was useless to try."

"That's why he was so angry that morning?" Gabriel asked.

"Yes, that's why he sent you off, and I couldn't stop him. The days went by, and nothing happened," Mrs. McLain went on. "But Mac was sure something *would* happen. Then, when he was checking over his ammunition yesterdeay afternoon, he discovered that he and George had made a mistake when they divided the supplies George had brought from the fort — Mac had the wrong kind. It was late in the day for so long a trip, but he was afraid to wait — he decided to ride over to George's and exchange it. He said he'd try to be back before dark. I can't think what can have happened to him."

"Oh, plenty of things could have delayed him," Gabriel said. He couldn't think what they might be, exactly, but he felt he had to say something to comfort Jean's mother. Soon he rose to his feet.

"What are you going to do?" Jean asked.

"I'm going to climb to the top of the ridge," he answered. "I want to see where the Cayuses have gone."

"And leave us here alone?"

"I have to. We must know where they are. And you must watch and listen. Remember our old signal — the mourning dove's call? One call means *Listen*. Two means *Danger — hide*. Three means *Come!* Can you remember?"

"I'll remember!" Jean promised. "But — come back soon!"

18

DANGER AHEAD

GABRIEL WAS OFF THEN, up the rocky hillside. It was still shadowy, but it would soon be full daylight. He kept to the cover of rock plants and boulders, finding a footing as best he could, pulling himself up with his hands where he had to.

Looking back, he could see sections of the trail as it wound along beside the creek. Jean and her mother and little Brian, he was glad to discover, were well out of sight.

He climbed steadily until he was near the top of the ridge. Then, under cover of a thicket of juniper, he sat down to rest and watch and listen.

Overhead the sky was silver blue with islands of rosy cloud moving slowly northward. To the southwest, the way he had come, the rocky ground fell

away into the shadows of the canyon. The trail
looked tiny now, winding along beside the white ribbon of Phantom Creek. Where the trail reached the
top end of the canyon it divided into three forks.
The main fork wound up a grassy rock-strewn slope,
and finally disappeared from sight over a ridge.

To the northeast the ridges climbed to a sweep of
high open country, cut through by stream beds winding toward the river. Still more distant rose the mountains, ridge upon ridge — green in the near distance,
deepending to dark blue, and at last to hazy purple
against the dawn sky.

Gabriel's eyes searched the landscape for a sign
that would reveal the Cayuses' position. The stream
beds were still in shadow, but the sun touched the
tops of the ridges. He could see nothing but the drifting shadows of the clouds floating high above.

He strained his ears, sifting the early morning
sounds. Chickadees called to one another from the
junipers, a note of sadness in their call now at summer's end. A chipmunk chattered in the pines down
the ridge. A little blue lizard appeared from nowhere
and sunned himself on a rock.

No hoofbeats from the trail below. No signal call
from Jean.

Again the boy's eyes swept the country. There —
what was that? Horses? Horses!

The wild band Flash had come from? No — there

132

were riders. They were far away, dark shapes angling up across a slope covered with sun-dried grass and sagebrush. They disappeared behind a ridge, then came up again on a farther slope.

They were in the clear now, single file. Gabriel counted — three, four, five. The five Cayuses! They seemed to be following a trail, though Gabriel could not see it. Once more they disappeared. He did not see them again.

But by and by, from back of the ridge, he saw the faintest thread of smoke rising in the clear air. Only a pale shadow against the dark trees beyond, and soon blown away by the breeze. But across Gabriel's face spread the first grin it had known for a long time. The Cayuses had given them up and stopped to fish and eat. He hoped the fishing was good! Tired, full Cayuses might sleep all day.

Gabriel started down the ridge. The sun was growing warmer. He'd be glad to reach the creek and a long, cool drink. But he'd better not be careless, he told himself, just because the Cayuses were far away. There might be others. So he kept eyes and ears open as he climbed back down the slope.

A flight of goldfinches, the sighing of the wind through the trees — that was all. Staying carefully out of sight from the trail, he climbed down almost to the glade by the falls.

Listen! The call of the mourning dove! The signal

from Jean! One call. A long silence. Then the single call again. That meant "Listen!" Gabriel crouched beneath a dwarf juniper, listening with bated breath. He could hear nothing.

Then again the single call from Jean. Nothing else.

He was in good cover now, far down the ridge toward the glade. He kept moving softly, watching the few loops of the trail that were in view. The trail was in sunshine now, the red soil pounded into fine dust by animals passing through the canyon. The dust lay undisturbed in the sunlight.

No! Above the farthest scrap of trail he could see, away through the trees, a tiny floating cloud of red dust! He strained his ears. Hoofbeats! More Cayuses?

He must be sure Jean and her mother and Brian and the horses were out of sight. With great caution he slipped down to within thirty yards of the bottom of the ridge and peered into the glade.

Mrs. McLain sat where he had left her, with Brian asleep in her lap. The horses were safe from view behind their thicket. Flattened against the trunk of a hemlock, almost invisible in her brown dress, Jean stood peering intently up the trail. The branches were thick around her — Gabriel doubted that she could see very much.

Once more Jean gave the dove signal. After a moment Gabriel echoed it to let her know that he had heard. She turned her head, but he was hidden from her. The hoofbeats were more distinct now. At least two horses, Gabriel guessed. Best not to move until they had passed. He saw that Jean had crouched low behind her tree, out of sight.

So thick was the growth of hemlock and juniper where Gabriel was hiding that he could see only one loop of the trail, and that nearly obscured by the trees. He fixed his eyes on the spot. He had made a mistake in coming so far down the slope. But it was too late now. He dare not move.

The hoofbeats blended with the sound of falling water. Then they grew louder, plainer. Gabriel's eyes were fixed on that one visible bend in the trail.

A horse and rider rounded the bend, appeared, and in a moment were gone, leaving only a puff of dust. An Indian? He couldn't say. In a moment, another horse and rider — no more distinct than the first. Nearer now, though unseen, the pounding hoofs ringing on the rocky trail. Strain as he would, Gabriel could not catch another glimpse of the riders.

The sound grew louder below him, passed, grew fainter as the riders continued up the trail. If only he could see!

From a higher spot, perhaps he could see the riders as they climbed the last mile before they reached the tablelands at the upper end of the canyon. Up he scrambled, over rough boulders and scrubby bushes.

He could follow the riders now, by the faint cloud of dust rising along the trail and drifting up through the trees. They had not yet reached the open spot. Gabriel fixed his eyes on it. The view was clear. Soon he would know!

There — a flicker of movement through the trees! Now the riders were in the open.

Gabriel gave a startled gasp. Then he went tearing down the mountainside.

"Jean! Mrs. McLain! It's Mac — on a strange horse. And Mr. Wright! They're on the trail of the Cay-uses!"

19

THE
TERRIBLE
MISUNDERSTANDING

MRS. MCLAIN JUMPED to her feet, startling Brian awake.

"Are you sure?" she cried. "Is Mac all right?"

"Looked to be. But I'll have to stop them. They'll trail the Indians, thinking they've captured you and Jean. They'll ride right into them!"

Already Gabriel had bridled Flash. Now he leaped to his back. The young stallion was fresh and full of life. He snorted and tossed his head as they swung up the trail, his mane flowing gold in the sunlight.

Up the trail they sped, now in sunshine, now in the deep shade of overhanging rocks or dark firs. There was a faint smell of dust in the air. Mac and George Wright were not far ahead. The canyon widened, the land flattened out.

Soon Gabriel and Flash were in the sunlight, at the bottom of a boulder-strewn slope. Here the trail forked. It took only a moment to find the marks of shod horses on the center trail.

Gabriel angled up the slope at a trot and topped the ridge. There — down the trail. George Wright was in the lead now, Mac a few paces behind him on the strange horse.

Gabriel shouted after them. They did not hear. He kicked Flash with his heels, and the sorrel shot forward. Again he shouted, waving an arm.

They heard! Mac turned in his saddle. What happened then was a nightmare.

Mac's hand flew to the rifle at his side. He was aiming at Gabriel! Aghast, the boy pulled Flash up short — and stood there, a perfect target against the sky.

There was a spurt of flame. Flash jumped, shied. A roar filled Gabriel's ears, a blow like that of a giant fist hit his shoulder. He was falling — he clutched at the reins, but there was nothing there.

"So this is the way it ends!" he thought in the split second it took him to fall. A boulder came up at him. His head struck it. Then blackness. . . . He lay still, sprawled on the sun-dried grass. . . .

"Where are they? What have ye done with them?" Gabriel felt himself being shaken, roughly and

without stopping. Light swam before him — rocks — sky so blue it hurt his eyes.

"What have ye done with them? I should ha' known ye couldna' be trusted! I should ha' known ye'd go with the other savages!"

There was rage in Mac's voice—and a thick Scotch burr, and tears. But what he wanted, Gabriel could not make out. Mac's contorted face was a blur.

"Tell me what ye've done with them!" Mac shouted into the boy's face. Gabriel swallowed and tried to speak. No words came.

He heard a clatter of hoofs. Then Jean dropped beside him as if from the sky.

"What have you done to Gabriel?" she cried. Mac looked at her as though he saw a spirit, his face white.

"Jean — Jean!" he cried. "Are ye all right, lass?"

"To be sure I'm all right. But what have you done to Gabriel? Oh, I knew this would happen! I should have come sooner!" Jean was breathless and sobbing. "All at once it came to me — you'd think Gabriel had joined the Cayuses!"

"Your mother — where is your mother? And Brian?"

"They're safe — back there in the canyon. Gabriel saved us, Father! We'd have been killed in our beds if it hadn't been for him! Gabriel and Flash!"

"And I shot him!" Mac breathed it softly. They

were beside Gabriel now, Jean and her father. Two pair of blue eyes, Mac's under troubled black brows, Jean's framed by brown hair curling around her temples, looked down at him. Were they full of tears — or was it tears in Gabriel's own eyes, from the bright sky and the pain in his head?

He managed a crooked grin. He tried to speak, but no words came. Then blackness closed in again, and he lay still.

-20-

FRIENDS ONCE MORE

GABRIEL WAS NEVER SURE just how they reached the
McLain ranch. He had fuzzy memories of riding Flash
down the canyon trail, each footstep sending stabs of
pain through his shoulder. He remembered clinging
desperately to Flash's mane, and riding into the setting sun with the light burning in his eyes.

Mac was there with a steadying hand. Mrs. McLain
was somewhere in the picture, and Jean and Brian on
Blackbird, and George Wright.

In bed in the loft of the McLain cabin he slept, and
woke, and slept again. Dreams came and went — fantastic dreams of the captain on a golden burro, and a
dark-eyed woman singing a lullaby, and a giant Cayuse coming after him on a painted pony.

When he wakened there were terrific burning

thrusts of pain in his shoulder. Mrs. McLain changed
the bandage and put on something wet and hot. Again
he sank into that half-real world between sleeping
and waking. In the half-wakeful hours, when people
came and went, Gabriel heard snatches of talk. Little
by little he pieced together the story of that eventful
night.

Mac had left George Wright's about sundown, riding his saddle horse Duke, and carrying the ammunition. Of course, he'd been in a hurry—too much of a
hurry. On the flat near the river, Duke had stepped in
a gopher hole and gone down. When he managed to
get to his feet, he was so lame he could scarcely put
his right front foot to the ground. Mac knew he
couldn't ride him the eight or ten miles home. So he
led him back to Wright's, intending to borrow George's
spare saddle horse.

George was willing, but the horse wasn't. The skittish Indian pony had slipped past the men and out of
the corral. George had chased him halfway up the
valley on his own horse before he caught him. By the
time the men got him back to Wright's, and Mac got
Duke's saddle and bridle on him, it was near midnight.

He had gone no more than a mile when George,
riding hard, overtook him. A young fellow from farther up the valley had brought news that a bunch of
young Cayuses were on the rampage — the same

Cayuses of which Pierre had warned Gabriel. George stayed with Mac, and they rode fast for the cabin. When they got there, it was empty.

They wasted precious time trying to discover what had happened. Had Mrs. McLain somehow learned of the Indians' approach, they wondered? Had she taken the children and hidden out with them somewhere in the foothills? Could they be in the loft of the big sheepshed? Or in the barn?

The two men had searched the ranch buildings, growing more frantic by the minute. In the barn, they discovered that Blackbird and Dolly were missing.

By torchlight — for the moon had long since gone down — they examined the tracks that led from the barn. It was Mac who discovered footprints of Indian ponies mingled with those of the two saddle mares.

"They've been captured by the Cayuses! The wretches have carried off my family and stolen my horses!" Mac had cried. Sharp in his mind was the memory of those terrified pioneer women and children he had helped rescue from the Indians on the plains, years before.

Dawn was breaking before the two men could make certain that the trail leading into the canyon was the one the Cayuses had taken. Mac's heart was filled with the blackest of thoughts as they tracked the Cayuse ponies through the canyon. When he had seen Gabriel racing after them on Flash, his first thought had been that the Indian boy had betrayed his loved ones to the Cayuses.

Turning it all over in his mind, Gabriel was almost surprised to find that his old resentment against the big Scotsman had vanished. Mrs. McLain and Jean and little Brian were safe—that was what mattered.

At last the morning came when Gabriel woke with a clear head and an urge to be up. It was early. The first shafts of sunlight from the east slanted through the little window in the end of the loft. All was quiet below.

Favoring his bandaged shoulder, Gabriel slipped on his clothes. The gay beaded leggings and jacket were dusty and rumpled, and there was a discolored hole in the shoulder. But it was good to be dressed again, and on his feet.

Quietly, so as not to waken the sleeping family, Gabriel slipped down the ladder and out the cabin door. His legs were a little shaky by the time he reached the corral. But his first whistle brought Flash to the bars, head up, whinnying. Gabriel slipped his hands under the flowing mane and laid his cheek against the soft nose.

"It's good to see ye out, lad!"

Gabriel jumped, startled at Mac's voice. He had not seen him come from the barn with the milk pail. He looked up, not sure what to say.

"Gabriel," Mac said, setting down the pail, "Sarah says I'm a stubborn man. Since the first day you came here she's told me I shouldna' be judging you from the tales I've heard, or what I've known of other Indians. But I was suspicious. I wouldna' trust you. And when I got home to find the cabin empty and my wife and bairns gone — carried away, as I thought, by the Cayuses — I told myself I'd been right.

"My thoughts got blacker every mile we went, following the trail up the canyon and out onto the mountain beyond. Then you were riding after us, and shouting.

"I didn't stop to think whether you were friend or enemy. All I could think was that you were one of the redskins who'd carried off my wife and little ones. You know the rest.

"It's — it's little enough a man can say to one who's saved his family's lives. Sarah and Jean told me all about how you came to warn us. I'm — I'm no speech maker. But I thank ye from the bottom of my heart, and I beg you'll forgive me that I so badly misjudged ye."

Gabriel held out his hand.

"It's all past," he said. "And it was Flash who found a safe place. We'd never have escaped the Cayuses if he hadn't led us into that little glade behind the

146

Gabriel slid off the sorrel's back and stood for a moment with his hand on the horse's silky neck. Suddenly a deep sense of gratitude filled his heart — gratitude for friends like the McLains and Lars and the captain, for parents who had loved him, for the wild and beautiful land he knew as home.

And for Flash. Perhaps most of all for Flash, his dream horse who had more than fulfilled all his dreams — who, with strength, loyalty, and uncanny animal wisdom, had shared with him the secret of Phantom Canyon.